APRIL'S KISS IN THE MOONLIGHT

JEAN C. JOACHIM

A Moonlight Series Novel

work is illegal. Criminal copyright infringement, including infringement without monetary gain, is investigated by the FBI and is punishable by up to 5 years in federal prison and a fine of $250,000.

A Moonlight Books sweet romance
Edited by Tabitha Bower
Proofread by Renee Waring
Cover design: Dawne Dominique
Copyright 2011 Jean C. Joachim

Moonlight Books

Dedication

To my special friends in the summer community at Lake Huntington, New York. Thank you for your support and good wishes and in appreciation of Lake Huntington, one of the most beautiful places to live.

Acknowledgment and special thanks for your help, expertise, support, ideas and genuine love and caring enabling me to write this book with accuracy and to do it twice! Lydia W. Stofka, Derek "Top Gun" Odom, Simon Smith-Wilson, Marilyn Lee, Diana Finegold, Sally Gallagher and Elizabeth Smythe.

Books by Jean C. Joachim

BOTTOM OF THE NINTH
DAN ALEXANDER, PITCHER
MATT JACKSON, CATCHER (Coming)
JAKE LAWRENCE, THIRD BASEMAN (Coming)
FIRST & TEN SERIES
GRIFF MONTGOMERY, QUARTERBACK
BUDDY CARRUTHERS, WIDE RECEIVER
PETE SEBASTIAN, COACH
DEVON DRAKE, CORNERBACK
SLY "BULLHORN" BRODSKY, OFFENSIVE LINE
AL "TRUNK" MAHONEY, DEFENSIVE LINE
HARLEY BRENNAN, RUNNING BACK
OVERTIME, THE FINAL TOUCHDOWN
A KING'S CHRISTMAS (Coming)
THE MANHATTAN DINNER CLUB
RESCUE MY HEART
SEDUCING HIS HEART
SHINE YOUR LOVE ON ME
TO LOVE OR NOT TO LOVE
HOLLYWOOD HEARTS SERIES
IF I LOVED YOU
RED CARPET ROMANCE
MEMORIES OF LOVE
MOVIE LOVERS
LOVE'S LAST CHANCE

LOVERS & LIARS
His Leading Lady (Series Starter)
<u>NOW AND FOREVER SERIES</u>
NOW AND FOREVER 1, A LOVE STORY
NOW AND FOREVER 2, THE BOOK OF DANNY
NOW AND FOREVER 3, BLIND LOVE
NOW AND FOREVER 4, THE RENOVATED HEART
NOW AND FOREVER 5, LOVE'S JOURNEY
NOW AND FOREVER, CALLIE'S STORY (prequel)
<u>MOONLIGHT SERIES</u>
SUNNY DAYS, MOONLIT NIGHTS
APRIL'S KISS IN THE MOONLIGHT
UNDER THE MIDNIGHT MOON
MOONLIGHT & ROSES (prequel)
<u>LOST & FOUND SERIES</u>
LOVE, LOST AND FOUND
DANGEROUS LOVE, LOST AND FOUND
<u>NEW YORK NIGHTS NOVELS</u>
THE MARRIAGE LIST
THE LOVE LIST
THE DATING LIST
<u>SHORT STORIES</u>
SWEET LOVE REMEMBERED
TUFFER'S CHRISTMAS WISH
THE SECOND PLACE HEART (Coming)

APRIL'S KISS IN THE MOONLIGHT

Chapter One

AS APRIL MCKENNA DROVE her small car around the bend and approached a tiny town, a good looking, big man with short, reddish brown hair stepped into the street and stuck out his thumb.

"Yeah, right, Mr. Serial Killer, like I'm going to give *you* a ride," she said aloud to herself, speeding up to pass him but unable to rip her gaze from his.

She averted her eyes, trying to focus on sorting out her life. Driving the back roads from Willow Falls, NY to her home in San Francisco would give April time to think. She had finished her MBA and was heading back for an internship in her father's company. The prelude to a staid, boring, corporate life worried her. The thought of such a future left her restless, unhappy. April didn't want to go back, didn't want to live her father's life. She wanted to break out, but didn't know how. She'd always been a good girl, doing the right thing, exactly what her parents expected of her.

With her mind occupied, she was driving on automatic pilot and noticed the glass scattered in the road too late. Her tire lasted another half mile before it blew. She pulled onto a muddy shoulder and got out of the car. She rummaged around in the car trunk having no idea where the spare tire or the jack were or even how to use them if she found them. She pulled out her cell phone only to remember she'd forgotten to recharge it before leaving school. Then she laughed when she realized there was no one to call anyway. *You're supposed to hang something white on the door handle when you need help.* April returned to the car, took off her white lace panties, the only white object she had, hung them on the door handle, closed the door and waited.

Only a few houses dotted the lonely country road, but acre after acre of green fields blossomed with ripe crops. Standing on tiptoe, she could barely make out a farmhouse in the distance. The tall corn stalks of late July blocked her car from view.

Half an hour passed and no car came by. Was she about to spend the night there in her car? Then she saw him in the rear view mirror. It was Mr. Serial Killer, coming around the bend, and heading straight for her car. Panic rose in her chest as she locked all the doors and hunkered down.

He walked up to the car and knocked on the window, startling April, who jumped. When she turned to look, he was smiling.

"Flat?" He asked.

She nodded.

"Pop the trunk." He headed for the rear of the car.

Can't you get inside the car through the trunk? He could attack me...

"Take it easy. I'm not a mass murderer. I'll change your tire."

April unlatched the trunk. If she didn't want to spend the night alone in the dark, accepting his help was her only choice.

"Are these yours?" he asked, plucking her panties off the door handle and holding them up to the car window. The white lace bikinis appeared to shrink in his large hand.

Heat seeped into April's her face. Avoiding the stranger's gaze, she cracked open the car window and snatched the garment from him. He laughed, shook his head and headed for the trunk, as she struggled to put them back on while sitting in the front seat.

"It's easier to jack up the car if you're not in it."

Reluctantly, she got out of the car, keeping an eye on him and perched on a large rock hugging her knees to her chest.

"Rusty," he said, extending his hand after taking off his backpack.

"April," she responded, wrinkling her nose at the sight of the grime coating his hand.

"Oh, yeah, sorry. Grease." He wiped his hand on his jeans.

He worked for forty-five minutes, jacking up the car then changing the tire. April watched in silence. As the sun beat down on him, he began to sweat. Rusty removed his T-shirt. April stared at his strong chest covered with reddish hair, feeling a desire to touch it. The muscles in his arms worked as he attached the jack and began to pump it up, moving the car higher and higher. He was tall, about six foot four inches, broad and strong. He shot her an easy grin from time to time.

"What's a beautiful girl like you doing stranded out here? Where you headed?" He asked, looking her over with appreciation in his eyes.

"San Francisco. You?" She said, blushing slightly under his gaze.

"I've got a week to get to Allentown for a job. At the rate I'm going, it'll take me a week to walk it." He worked the tire iron on the lug nuts.

She laughed. "Why kind of job?"

"Driving a truck to New York City and back. It pays well."

"You going to live in Allentown?"

"Of course. Where are you coming from?"

"Got my MBA from Kensington State University. Heading home."

"Going back to a job?"

"Uh...an internship. But I don't want to. I'm not sure what I want to do."

"After all that time with college and graduate school and you still don't know what you want to do? Heck...a lot of money down the drain."

"Education doesn't always tell you what you want to do in life."

"True enough. Still going home, eh?" He leaned against the car.

"It's expected."

"Car's ready. You should replace the dead tire because if this one blows, you're out of luck," he pointed out, putting his shirt back on.

"Thanks. Get in," she said, standing up, and brushing herself off.

"You giving me a ride?"

She shrugged and gave a nod.

"Well, I can promise not to strangle and murder you... but I might kiss you," he said.

"Thanks for fixing the tire. I'm taking you all the way to Allentown," she said.

"No way! You are? Fantastic."

"The least I can do...it's not far out of my way and...I'm in no hurry."

"Up for a little journey?" he asked her with a wicked grin on his face.

"Maybe." She looked him over, thinking about his offer of adventure.

"Let's get some food. There's a diner down the road a ways and I'm buying," he said, holding the door open for her.

She smiled up at him as he closed the car door.

APRIL OPENED HER EYES and sat up, not totally aware of her surroundings. She was in the back seat of a car and it had been ten months since she'd met Rusty on the side of the road. Terrible pain tore through her midsection whenever she moved.

"You're up?" the woman driving the car said.

"Where am I?"

"Heading toward Pine Grove. I'm Sunny Foster, your mom's friend. I picked you up at the hospital an hour ago?"

April's head was fuzzy. She lay back down on the seat and closed her eyes; her dreams began. She saw her car with Rusty behind the wheel. She was walking...no running toward the car. There was a click, then an explosion. Debris went airborne, then a plastic garbage can came flying at her. She put up her arms to fend it off, but the force of the can slamming into her arms turned them into weapons, breaking one rib and bruising two more. The can knocked her on the ground where her head hit hard, she lost consciousness.

Rusty! Rusty's dead. Yeah, Rusty's dead. April's eyes fluttered open again for a few seconds then closed again, as she tried to disappear into sleep. It was too soon for her to face the truth about the horrible accident.

Chapter Two

She slept until Sunny pulled up in front of a large Victorian house, where Sunny's husband, Mike, was waiting to help her out of the car. When the car stopped, April smiled weakly at the couple. She checked her wrist. The shimmering, glittery narrow band was still there. The band-turned-bracelet was made from the collar of her beloved cat, Sasha. When the cat died at fifteen, five years earlier, her mother fashioned a bracelet out of the collar for April, and she rarely took it off.

Mike picked up her suitcase and hauled it into the guest room on the first floor. April, grimacing in pain, slid out of the car with Sunny's help.

"I have a prescription for pain meds I'll get filled for you. In the meantime, your doctor gave me some medication. Let's get inside so you can take it."

April climbed the stairs slowly.

"Would it help if I carried you?" Mike asked.

He went over and picked her up but put her down quickly when she screamed in pain. Taking the stairs slowly, April was able to make it into the kitchen. She smelled a fragrant pot of fresh coffee brewing while Sunny made lunch. The homey smell warmed her and made her feel welcome. They all sat down to eat. April was banged up with a black eye, cuts and bruises on her face, shoulders and chest, one wrist was in a small cast. Adding to the insult, she'd also suffered a concussion.

"What happened to you?" Mike asked, taking a swig of his coffee, trying not to stare at April.

"An explosion...I was too close," she said, quickly, not wishing to re-live it.

Sunny handed her two pills and pushed a glass of water over to her.

"Your mom was my mentor when I was studying art at Kensington State, quite a while ago," Sunny said.

"She called you?" April put the pills in her mouth then washed them down with a gulp of water.

"The hospital called her and I'm much closer, so she called me. We're happy to have you here with us, April...wish it was under different circumstances," Sunny said, taking April's hand.

Her finger came up against a ring on April's finger. She glanced at it.

"You were engaged? To whom?"

"Rusty." April shifted in her seat as tears clouded her eyes. "He asked me to marry him about a week before the explosion," she explained.

"Your mom didn't tell me you lost your fiancé."

"She doesn't know."

"You didn't tell her you were engaged?"

"They wouldn't have liked Rusty, and now...it doesn't matter," She said, two tears slipping down her cheek.

Sunny was overwhelmed with emotion and gave April a gentle hug.

"Stay with us as long as you need to, April," Mike said.

"Thank you. I don't know what I would have done without you two," she said.

April spent most of the next week sleeping. When she was awake she was weepy, thinking about Rusty and her life, writing her thoughts and feelings in her diary. While she was in bed, Missy, Mike's black lab mix lay down on the floor next to her bed and Trixie, Sunny's pug climbed into bed with April, curling up next to her legs. Missy licked the tears off April's face. Crying made her ribs hurt, so she tried hard to control her emotions, with help from the dogs who often were silly enough to make her laugh, which caused equal pain.

MILES AWAY, IN ALLENTOWN, Juan, a short man in his early forties, with a black mustache, sat in a booth in Googie's Diner facing his friend, Caleb. Caleb, younger than his friend, was tall and lean, with cold, gray eyes. The remnants of their meal of burgers and fries littered the table.

Caleb added more sugar to his coffee while Juan sucked down a soft drink. He put the glass down and pointed to a newspaper, lying flat, open to page three.

"Says here, our guy, Rusty, was killed when his car exploded," he said, lifting his gaze to meet his friend's.

"Yeah? Rusty's dead?" Caleb cocked an eyebrow.

"That's what it says."

"So, where's the money? Caleb asked.

"Good question, my friend. Good question."

The waitress stopped by to drop off a check. Juan picked it up and reached in his back pocket.

"Let's go."

Caleb rose and followed his friend out the door.

BY THE MIDDLE OF THE second week, some strength returned to April and the bruises had started to fade. Saturday morning, she eased under a hot shower. The water soothed her aching body. Sounds of construction, louder than the shower spray, came from the room across the hall. In the car, Sunny had mentioned something about turning it into a nursery because they'd planned to have a child. April tried to think back to the exact words, but her memory of conversations on that ride was hazy.

After turning off the water, she dried her long, lustrous, dark brown hair. The locks fell to her shoulders in loose curls framing her oval face, beautiful before it became bruised. A peek in the mirror reflected troubled eyes, so dark they were almost black. Her shiner was turning yellow and the angry splotch on her delicate chin matched.

She wrapped a towel around her body and tucked the corner in between her breasts, picked up her hair dryer and opened the bathroom door. She walked down the hall and ran smack dab into the best looking man she'd ever seen, coming around the corner. She bumped into him and clutched her towel to secure it. He steadied her with big hands on her elbows as their gazes met. He stared, his eyes taking in every inch of the pretty girl. A sizzle, like an electric current, rose up her arms from his touch.

Rusty had been the only man in her life who could raise such heat in her veins. Now he was gone, so how could it happen again? She knit her brows for a moment, then shifted her weight, uncomfortable under his scrutiny. Who was this guy and why did he affect her when she didn't even know him?

Standing about six feet tall with a slender, but powerful build, the intriguing stranger had the bluest eyes and darkest hair imaginable. His eyebrows were thick, sideburns perfectly clipped and two-days growth of beard appeared on his long, narrow face. She couldn't take her eyes off him.

It appeared the reaction was mutual. Obviously entranced, he'd been rendered speechless by her sultry, barely-clad, five feet four inches—normally attractive, now painfully colorful. His eyebrows lifted as he eyed her bruised shoulders.

"What happened to *you?*" he muttered, dropping his hands from her arms.

"Got in the way of an explosion," she explained, pulling her gaze away from his.

He nodded, then eyed the engagement ring on her hand. She twisted the yellow gold band with a small diamond chip. Touching the token from her dead lover brought him to mind. She needed to take off the ring. She was no longer engaged and the sooner she faced it the better.

"Gavin Dailey," he said, extending his hand.

"April McKenna."

She tightened her grip on the towel with one hand and extended the other to him. A sudden slip of the cover-up caused her to fold her arm across her chest, holding the towel in place. She managed to secure the towel's precarious tuck at her chest while her face flamed. Before it fell completely, April sputtered something unintelligible and ran from the room, followed by the sound of his low chuckle.

Once safely inside her room, she banged the door shut and leaned up against it. Her pulse quickened, she took a long, slow breath before removing the towel and searching for clean clothes. How could that man affect her this way? Sure he was great looking, but Rusty had only been dead a few days. How could this new guy ramp up her body with one long look?

Shame at her assumed disloyalty to Rusty burned in her heart. She took her lip between her teeth and went to the window. Clouds had gathered over the small town. What could she do now? Where would she live? Confusion mixed with fear and a sharp loneliness, bringing tears to her eyes.

But there wasn't time for self-pity. She needed to make some decisions and get on with her life. How could she? Didn't she deserve a period of mourning? She shrugged. Maybe it would be okay to stay at Sunny's for a while, until she got her bearings. She sighed as she watched three mixed breed dogs romp in the backyard.

GAVIN HAD BEEN TAPING the molding in the spare room before painting when his focus was interrupted by the squeaky hinge on the guest bedroom door. He spotted April. His eagle eye noticed she wasn't wearing her engagement ring. His gaze swept over her form offering frank male appreciation as she approached the back door. She glanced at him as she passed and he smiled. A small smile played at her lips before she turned away and continued on her path.

Gavin walked to the door, watching her take the steps to the yard. As soon as she hit the grass, a dog flanked her on each side while the third trotted ahead, as if making sure her way was safe.

His gaze lingered on the sway of her hips, then roamed up to the bounce of her hair as she loped along. The dogs took off, running, chasing each other. April started out after them, but stopped abruptly. She grabbed her calf as she fell to the ground. He started after her, but she pushed to her feet within moments of falling. She turned back to the house, her mouth turned down. He couldn't see tears, but swore she was in pain. He stood mesmerized. As if she could feel his gaze, she looked up at the window where he stood. April's fingers raked her hair as Gavin's eyes met hers. His breath stopped for a moment before he backed away and returned to work.

Peering around the open door, he spied April enter. She leaned against the wall by the back door, her head bent, her hand over her eyes. She raised one leg toward her chest. Her back expanded for a moment then went back to normal.

He winced, seeing her double over. He wanted to fold her in his arms, soothe her with kisses until each bruise disappeared. A slight heat crept into his cheeks when he remembered the engagement ring she had worn. Never before had he wanted another man's woman. What had happened to that ring? Did she simply take it off to wash her hands or did it mean more than that?

Warmth in his chest and a tingle in his arms to comfort her surprised him. Although his aunt and uncle had urged him to find a girl and settle down, Gavin was still searching. He'd dated every eligible female in the county and beyond. Or so it seemed. But none had measured up. His uncle Barney had teased him that his standards were so high a beauty pageant winner couldn't meet them.

Let them laugh at him. When Gavin Dailey tied the knot it would stay tied, forever. He'd make a lifetime commitment, but only to the right woman. At this point in his life, he'd never had the desire to stick around for more than a few months.

His buddies at the firehouse ragged him constantly about being a player and sleeping from one coast to the other. Gavin wanted more. He'd watched his aunt and uncle who'd been married forever. He wanted the rock solid love that they had. He wanted beauty, brains and loyalty. Only a women with that and more would be the one he'd choose.

Sure everyone he knew had fixed him up at one time or another. And he'd met a few young women who were worth his time. Always a measured man, he'd date a girl, get to know her before he'd decide. After all, that crap about chemistry was simply that –garbage, romantic nonsense.

He knew the truth –love had to build over time. It didn't strike you like lightning. Only fools believed that. At least that's what Gavin Daily thought. Until now.

AT DINNER TIME, APRIL helped set the table while Sunny and Mike made dinner and sang to each other, warming up for their evening performance. Mike had a steady gig at The Roadhouse on Friday and Saturday nights with a scruffy little band he'd put together and named Electricity. Some weekends, Sunny sang with him.

When Mike moved up behind Sunny and wound his arms around her waist, April found an excuse to turn away. After all they were newlyweds. She couldn't help peeking at them, even though embarrassment heated her cheeks. They didn't mean to disappear into each other, but sometimes they made her feel like a third wheel.

Their song was "Hello Again," a Neil Diamond song.

"Reminds me of how Sunny and I reconnected." Mike said.

"After not seeing each other for twenty years!" Sunny put in.

"We'd been friends. Sort of like big brother and little sister," he continued.

"Yeah, I was a real pest. Hard to imagine now," Sunny said.

Mike raise his eyebrows causing his wife to swat him with a dish towel. April guessed that their childhood affection other had finally blossomed into love. Married a little over a year, they wanted a family. Mike loved to joke about getting Sunny pregnant. While April shifted uneasily when he cracked some of his jokes because she didn't know the couple well, his wife merely laughed with him.

Before they left for The Roadhouse, Sunny applied cover up make-up to April's facial bruises. The young brunette wore a low cut red jersey dress and Sunny a dark blue one. They donned light coats as it was not yet May and still chilly in Pine Grove, a small town located in upstate New York.

When they got to the restaurant, the band was already seated at their usual table, anticipating meeting the new filly. Doobie, the tallest and youngest member of the band was wearing jeans, long-sleeved shirt and bow tie. Jack, the senior member was dressed in a green flannel shirt and jeans and Al, the shyest of the four, wore a blue and white plaid shirt, jeans and navy blue jacket.

The band members stood up when Sunny and April walked in. Mike made the introductions.

"Who beat *you* up?" Al asked April.

She looked at him with startled eyes, surprised by his frankness but made no reply.

"Al can't talk to women," Doobie joked.

"She was in an explosion," Sunny explained to Al.

The man in plaid with a slightly large nose blushed. "Sorry."

"It's all right, Al." April patted his forearm and chuckled.

She stopped laughing when she noticed Gavin standing near the table.

"Gavin! How nice to see you! Join us," Sunny offered.

"Do you know April?" Mike asked Gavin.

"You look different with your clothes on—" he began, then stopped talking and blushed furiously.

"She's only been here a ten days, Gavin. That's fast, even for you!" Mike snickered.

"She was in a towel...when I met her, I mean," he stammered.

"Gavin, pull up a chair," Sunny said, watching two faces turn red.

He grabbed one from another table and squeezed between Al and April, quietly moving his arm around the back of her chair.

"What did you have to invite him for, Sunny?" Al whined.

"Al, you don't stand a chance with a chick who looks like April anyway," Jack said.

"Not with him here," Al grumbled, pointing at Gavin.

The firefighter chuckled.

The waitress came over to their table. "Do y'all know what you want?"

The others ordered, then she got to Al.

"Give me the lonely man's special..." he said, resting his chin in his hands. (add 140)

THEY RETURNED HOME, tired and subdued. Mike took the dogs for a late night walk, then he and Sunny went to bed. April slipped between the sheets and stared out at the moon. But by two in the morning, April was still awake. She picked up her diary and went to the kitchen for a cup of tea while she recorded the events of the day. She put the kettle on, then sat at the table, scribbling away when Sunny tip-toed in.

"Couldn't sleep?" Sunny asked, drawing her robe tighter around her body.

She shook her head, closing her book.

"Rusty?" Sunny took down two mugs from the cabinet.

"Among other things." April opened a canister and retrieved two Earl Grey teabags.

Sunny raised an eyebrow.

"I've messed up. I was supposed to go home from Kensington, but I met Rusty and went to Allentown with him. We took a couple of days to get there, camping out under the moonlight together..." The whistle of the kettle drew April's attention.

"It sounds romantic," Sunny grinned.

"It was. He was so sweet I decided to stay with him. When I told my parents I wasn't coming back for a while, they went ballistic. I didn't tell them where I was or where I was going or when I was coming back. Mom got in the car to come after me but before she even got out of California, she was in an accident. She's still doing physical therapy. Dad blames me and I suppose it *is* my fault."

Sunny took April's hand.

"It isn't your fault."

"I'd been with Rusty since last July. We lived together and my parents hated it. So I stopped speaking to them. I got a new cell phone...and didn't give them the number. I wanted something different...to make my own choices. Now Rusty is dead. I'm alone. They hate me..." April stopped, emotion closing up her throat, tears stinging her eyes.

Sunny squeezed her hand.

"You're entitled to live your own life, April. You're not responsible for your mom's accident either. None of this is your fault and I'm sure your folks don't hate you. You're twenty-six? Old enough to make your own choices. Maybe you should talk to them."

"I can't. If I talk to them, they'll talk me into coming home with them...and being miserable. I'm not ready yet." April added sugar to her tea.

"Okay. You don't have to. I'm going to call your mom tomorrow with a report on how you're doing here. I'll tell them you're out or sleeping or something."

"Thank you."

A sleepy Mike entered the kitchen, and Sunny poured him a cup of tea.

"A tea party at this hour?"

"April couldn't sleep...neither could I."

"I could, until I found half the bed empty," he said.

He sat down next to Sunny and picked up his drink.

"Girl talk?" He asked.

April yawned. "Back to bed for me," she said, hugging Sunny, "thank you."

Mike stood up and took Sunny's hand.

"Since we're up..." he started, his eyes glistening.

"Try, try and try again, eh, Mike?" Sunny said, laughing.

"You read my mind," he replied, leading her back to the bedroom.

April heard a giggle as the couple padded down the hall and back to bed. She returned to the kitchen to clean up. After the last dish was put away, she yawned. She barely made it back to bed before falling into a deep sleep.

Chapter Three

April was up early. She fed the dogs and took them out back for a walk. Gavin arose at daybreak and sitting on the roof of the firehouse with binoculars, scanning the lake. He often went up there to watch for eagles and other raptors. This morning he couldn't find the majestic birds but he moved the binocs over to the old Victorian and spied April in the backyard with the dogs.

He descended the outside stairs and ambled over. She was sitting on a bench near the garden when he entered the gate.

"Howdy," he said, closing it behind him.

She jumped.

"Didn't mean to scare you." He eased down next to her.

"You don't scare me." He didn't believe her.

He stared at her lips for a moment, wondering what they'd taste like and how long he'd have to wait to find out.

"Don't *want* to scare you. If I wanted to...I could," he said, shooting her a wicked grin.

"Stop teasing," she said, petting Gus, the black Lab mix.

"Where is your ring?" His hand brushed hers when he scratched the mutt behind the ears.

"My ring? I'm not engaged anymore...so I took it off." She shrugged, rubbing around the base of her ring finger.

"Dumped the guy?"

"He died."

"Oh, I'm sorry, I didn't know," he said, putting his arm around her. *Open mouth, insert foot.*

"Look, farm boy..." She squirmed out of his embrace.

"I'm no farm boy."

"You're not? I suppose you're a world traveler?" She asked, arching an eyebrow.

"Might be—for all you know."

"I'm going to be, a world traveler. I'm moving on from this dusty place soon," she said, waving her hand to include the lush farmland and barn.

"Where you going?"

"I don't—I don't know...yet. But..." she stammered and blushed.

"I've been places..." He stared at the dog.

"Oh? Where? Oak Bend? Willow Falls?" She asked, arching an eyebrow, her hands on her hips.

"Paris."

"You've been to Paris?" She asked, pushing to her feet.

"Jealous?" He responded, standing and stepping closer to her.

"Maybe...a little," she said, coughing nervously, backing away from him, "what were you doing in Paris?"

"I studied there for two years, *Mademoiselle*," he said, walking up to her.

"*C'est vrai?*" She responded, moving away from him.

"*Bien sur, jeune fille,*" he retorted.

"I'm no *jeune fille*," she shot back, inching toward the tool shed.

"I'm no 'boy' either," he said, following her.

"What did you study in Paris, Farm Boy?" She moved close to the shed.

Gavin followed her, determined to make his point all the while drawn to her like a moth to a flame.

"I studied French language, culture, and." He slipped in front of her, forcing her back against the shed.

Gavin put a hand against the wall on either side of her head, and moved right up against her, his chest lightly touching hers. They were close enough he could smell the freshness of her newly washed hair, feel the warmth of her breath on his neck, close enough to kiss. Trying hard to resist her, he leaned down slightly, his lips barely touching her ear.

"and—how to make love to a woman," he whispered. "Would you like me to show you?"

His mouth only a fraction of an inch from her skin, he saw the pulse beat wildly in her throat. Her breathing quickened. He lowered his lips to barely brush her skin starting with the throbbing in her neck and skimming down slowly to her shoulder and back up again. She closed her eyes for a moment, then put her hands against this hard chest and shoved.

"I believe you," she gasped, moving away quickly, smoothing back her hair, her hands trembling slightly.

He laughed at her and pulled at the collar of his shirt. "No more 'farm boy'," he ordered.

"Okay, no more farm boy," she agreed, her dark chocolate eyes wide.

He followed her back to the bench and sat close to her. He bent his head again and inhaled deeply, closing his eyes.

"Thought I recognized it...spring roses," he said.

"What?"

"That's what you smell like. I'm going to call you 'Springtime'," he said.

"Why?"

"Because your name is April and you smell like spring roses," he said, standing up.

She looked up at him, her lips parted in a smile. "I've got fresh coffee inside."

"I've got work to do," he said, heading for the door.

"Suit yourself." She called to the dogs and followed him into the house.

By ten, Gavin, in old jeans worn in the knees and faded with a thousand washings and a black T-shirt, drew a paintbrush back and forth. He created a wide mint green border around the molding of the wall in Sunny's spare room. The fire fighter tried to concentrate on his work but the smell of spring roses stuck with him, despite the strong odor of fresh paint. He imagined the delicate scent everywhere he turned, expecting to see April but was disappointed.

When the fire alarm went off, the loud noise frightened all three dogs, which began to bark loudly. Gavin counted three short blasts and one long one. With a sigh, he put down his paintbrush.

"Mike!" he called, "I gotta go."

Gavin took long strides toward the door. April sat up in the living room where she was writing in her leather bound diary. She raised her eyebrows at him as if to ask where he was going.

"There's a fire...near Meadow Lane, three short, one long..." he said before he ran to his truck, threw it in gear and sped out of the driveway. He drove to the firehoouse in time to meet the truck. He stripped off his shirt and donned the fireman's coat waiting for him on a hook on the side.

Pete, the fire chief, was behind the wheel. Four more cars carrying volunteer firemen screeched to a halt. The men jumped on the truck then headed toward the burning building.

APRIL RECALLED MIKE telling her Gavin wasn't just a painter, but also a member of the Pine Grove fire department, too.

"Did Gavin leave?" Mike asked.

April nodded moving to the front door where she could get a better look at what was happening. With its siren blasting, the fire engine raced down the street. Firemen shrugged into their heavy black coats as the truck rumbled along.

Secretly, she admired his bravery to fight fires and rescue strangers. She didn't know much about it, but knew it was a dangerous job. Often the people who got hurt the most in a fire were those battling it. She put away her journal and went for a walk down to the lake. She could smell smoke in the air and followed the scent. It was a warm day for the beginning of May, and she was comfortable in only her T-shirt and jeans.

As she got closer to the smell, she saw a yellow farmhouse near the lake. Sunny had told April that Gavin lived there with his aunt and uncle. A slender woman with gray hair was sweeping the front porch—she must be Gavin's aunt. The fire engine came around the bend on its way back to the firehouse, and stopped in front of the yellow house to let Gavin off before speeding away. After a conversation with his aunt, Gavin headed around to the back of the house.

April approached quietly, then backed up, moving to the side where she could watch him without detection. Gavin stood at a faucet with the water running. Black soot stained his shirt and face. April hovered at the edge partially hidden by a copse of trees, watching as he took his shirt off and rinsed it out in the water, and then placed it on a large, flat stone. She felt awkward spying on him undressing, but he was too attractive for her to look away. She watched as he picked up a piece of soap and worked up a good lather in his hands. He scrubbed his head, then his pecs. Strong arm muscles worked as he soaped up the dark hair on his chest. He was beautifully formed, with strong broad shoulders that tapered to a narrow waist. His abs were developed but not like some overly-brawny weightlifter, they were firm but normal looking. She grew warm watching him, and tiny beads of sweat broke out on her forehead. The muscles in his back worked as he stretched to get himself clean. Then he ducked his head and chest under the faucet to rinse off.

April's lips were dry, her throat parched. She was mesmerized, drawn by his masculine beauty and unable to move or stop staring.

He reached for the button on his jeans and she panicked, realizing he was about to take off his pants. Blushing deeply, she turned to leave, stepping on a big twig which snapped under her foot. He stopped immediately and turned around. A big grin appeared on his face as he spied her, through the shrubbery, making her getaway.

"Hey, April! Where you going?" He hollered over to her as he grabbed a towel and began drying his torso.

April was too embarrassed to speak and froze where she was while he made his way over to her.

"What are you doing over here?" He asked her.

"Following the fire, until..."

"You got distracted watching me get undressed, huh?" He said, laughing at her.

"I...I...didn't know what..." she stuttered, feeling more heat creep into her face.

"It's okay, Springtime. I'm glad you're here," he said softly, moving closer to her.

Her eyes grew wide as he got closer.

"Aunt Laura doesn't like me to come into the house directly from a fire. Says I bring the smoke smell inside with me. So I undress out back, rinse out my clothes and then go in. You stopped me before the show got good," he snickered.

"I didn't mean to...I never would have...really had no idea..."

He laughed. "I don't mind you watching me undress...as long as you return the favor some time." He joked, his gaze moving over her body with obvious admiration.

Her humiliation grew so strong, tears welled up, which he saw moments before she turned away, hiding her eyes with her hand.

"I'm sorry. I didn't mean to upset you," he said, drawing her into his arms for a hug.

Her hands slid over the rock-hard muscles in his arms and onto his shoulders as he pulled her closer. The scent of pine soap mixed with a hint of smoke greeted her nostrils as she buried her burning face in his shoulder. He held her silently for several minutes until she regained her composure. When she stepped back and looked up at him, he lowered his lips to hers for a gentle kiss. At the touch of his lips, desire rose in her chest and when she didn't resist, he deepened the kiss and crushed her against him.

"Gavin!" Aunt Laura called from the back porch, raising her hand to her eyes to shield them from the sun.

He let April go, stepped out from behind the large bush concealing them, and waved at his aunt. She waved back. When April came out from behind the bush and hid behind Gavin, Laura stopped and focused her sixty-year-old eyes on the girl. She stared hard in their direction but finally shook her head.

"Who's that with you?" she called.

"New friend," Gavin shouted back.

"It's too cold to be out like that," she yelled.

"Gotta go," he said, turning toward April. "Remember now, you promised to return the favor."

April's face flamed. "I did not!"

Gavin gave her a wicked grin. "Can't blame me for trying," he shot back at her as he started to jog to the house. Air cooled April's skin where it had been warmed by the pressing of his body. She shivered and folded her arms across her chest.

AFTER HE RETURNED TO the yellow house, Gavin watched April walk away. He ran his tongue over his bottom lip, tasting her sweet flavor again. Her scent lingered on his skin, enticing him, making him want her in a way he hadn't wanted a woman in a long time. She was the prettiest and the feistiest woman he'd ever met. No way was April falling all over herself to curry favor with him. He liked her independence, the challenge she presented. His resolve to win her, no matter what, hardened. Smart, beautiful women with their own minds didn't grow on trees in Pine Grove. Gavin wanted to settle down and have a family and April McKenna suited his taste to a tee.

When he got inside, Aunt Laura took his clothes and dumped them in the washing machine. "Who was that I saw you with?"

"I told you, a new friend."

"Hah! Expect me to believe that? You don't hide behind a bush with a friend, Gavin Dailey, so stop shootin' the crap with me. Who is she?"

"She's staying at The Fosters...daughter of a friend of Sunny's, I think. Her name is April McKenna."

"Pretty?"

"Very." He smiled at the memory of April's obvious embarrassment at being caught watching him strip down and the delicious kiss they'd shared.

"Of course. Should've known. So how well do you know her? Are you two an item?"

"Aunt Laura! Don't you think you should stop these inquisitions now...I'm thirty."

"Laura, leave Gavin be," her husband, Barney, said, filling the door-way to the kitchen with his bulky self.

"Okay, okay. A body likes to know what's going on is all," she said, turning on the washer and leaving the room.

"So, Gavin, you got a new filly in the stable?" Barney asked his nephew.

"Barney...drop it."

"Heck, your love life is the spice of my day," Barney sighed.

"Maybe you'd better do something about your life, Barney," Gavin joked.

"If you're suggesting a new woman, Laura Dailey is all the woman I need...or can handle!"

Gavin went up to the third floor, which Barney and Laura had turned into a bachelor apartment. He showered, put on fresh clothes and picked up his binoculars to if the eagle living by the lake was out fishing for his lunch. While he stood, patiently awaiting the majestic bird, he reflected on his life.

He'd lived in France with his Aunt Felice for two years after her husband died. She didn't want to be alone, so she invited Gavin to stay. They got along beautifully. He also charmed her friends and was often invited to parties and dinners at their homes. He'd grown up during his stay in Paris, and learned how to be a man of the world. But when Laura and Barney called on the family for help after Barney broke his leg, Gavin had volunteered to move to Pine Grove and live with them, to help manage their farm.

Grateful for his help, especially after the death of their only child, Joe, in Iraq, Barney and Laura went out of their way to make Gavin's life on the farm comfortable. His apartment was charming but the hand-made bookcase, attractive country curtains and matching bedspread couldn't make up for the fact he lived alone, and slept alone most nights. He joined Laura and Barney for meals and they never bothered him when he was entertaining a young lady.

Barney, who'd married young, lived vicariously through his nephew's exploits. He loved to hear about Gavin's girlfriends and from time to time when they were working together on the farm, Gavin would share some of his experiences. Too much of a gentleman to reveal personal details, Gavin did tell Barney enough though to keep him coming back for more. Gavin was close to his uncle and sometimes asked him for advice.

The best present they'd given their nephew was a two-acre plot on Beacon Lane. Gavin started building a log home there in his spare time. He loved Pine Grove, the life, the people and planned to settle there. This would be where he'd raise his family, he'd decided. Barney told him if he built a house, he and Laura would pay for plumbing and electrical work. So the young man sawed, hammered and measured most every weekend when he wasn't on duty at the firehouse. Although at first he'd been disconcerted by April's attitude, he believed if she stayed there long enough, she'd fall in love with the place like he did. All that remained would be making her fall in love with him, too, usually not a difficult task for Gavin...but maybe not so easy this time.

Chapter Four

On Sunday, Mike, Sunny and April took the members of the band with them to the Farmer's Fair in Willow Falls. The fair showcased animals and other 4-H exhibits, offered a variety of rides and all kinds of carnival food. Mike was looking to buy two more dairy cows for his small farm. Local teens raised farm animals and sold them at the Farm Fair every year. The band was tagging along for the experience, none of them having been to an event like this before.

They paid the three-dollar entry fee, and were immediately assaulted by the seductive smells of carnival food. The aroma of frying onions, sizzling funnel cakes, cheese steaks, corn roasting on the grill, enticed them toward the food booths. April's stomach growled at her first sniff.

"Cheese steak, corn or chicken on a stick?" Doobie asked Jack and Al.

"All three!" Al responded.

"You guys can scatter since you won't be looking at cows..."

"Women...looking for women..." Al broke in.

"Whatever. Meet us back here at the admission booth at four o'clock," Mike said.

"April, you can come with us if you like," Sunny offered.

"I'm starving. I'll meet you by the cows after I eat," she said, moving off.

Drawn to the funnel cake booth, she watched the batter pour slowly out of the funnel into the pan full of spitting, hot grease, then turn golden brown. The man behind the booth turned it once, then picked it up with tongs and dumped it into a plate of powdered sugar. The smell was intoxicating and April salivated.

"I bet you've never eaten one of those, City Girl."

She turned her head to see Gavin standing behind her in line. She shook her head and turned back to watch the man pour the next funnel cake, her funnel cake and watch it cook.

"They are as delicious as they look," Gavin whispered in her ear.

April's mouth watered as she watched the man, totally bored with his task, go through the motions as he'd probably done hundreds of times that day. He took her four dollars and handed over the hot funnel cake on a paper plate. She burned her fingers trying to pick it up.

"The trick is to wait for it to cool off enough so you can pick it up without letting it get so cold the grease gets disgusting," Gavin said, watching his funnel cake while maintaining eye-contact with April.

She sucked on her burned fingers. Gavin took her hand and wrapped her fingers around his ice cold bottle of water, then pulled out his money for the man.

"Thank you," she said bashfully, holding the water bottle with her injured hand.

"What are you doing here?" He steered her to an empty picnic table and sat down.

"Mike wants to look at some dairy cows," she said.

Gavin nodded.

"What kind of animals do they have here?" asked April.

"All kinds. Mostly farm animals, but some rabbits and guinea pigs, too. And horses."

"Where are they?"

Gavin, chewing on his funnel cake, gestured toward the back of the fairgrounds.

April sighed as Al caught her eye and wandered over, the rest of the band in tow.

"Crap! Dailey how do you always find her first? You got April radar or something?" Al whined.

"Always, for a pretty woman," answered Gavin with a grin in Al's direction.

"Nuts!" Al said, then took a big bite of his cheese steak.

Doobie and Jack spread out their food, burgers, three ears of corn on the cob, curly fries, sweet potato fries and three large beers.

"Will you join us, April?" Jack asked.

"Maybe...just half a burger," she said, shyly.

"Please, help yourself," Al said, pushing a burger her way.

April ate it slowly, having filled up on the greasy funnel cake. The band members argued about a new song while they ate. Gavin finished his funnel cake and sat quietly.

"Want to see the animals," he asked, holding his hand out to April when she finished the last of the burger.

She nodded, flashing a smile in his direction.

"Geesh! Come on Dailey! Wait till we finish," Al protested.

"Why Al? Can you tell her something...anything about goats, rabbits or horses?"

"Well...maybe not, but still I'd like to go along..."

"Why?"

"Because you're monopolizing her. I saw her first."

"Actually I saw her first...in fact more of her than you've ever seen. I'll bring her back in one piece, Al, and you can make your play then." Tossing the other man a victorious half-grin, Gavin took April's hand, pulling her away from the table.

"Thanks for the burger, guys," she said, waving.

They nodded. Al was the only one not smiling.

APRIL AND GAVIN STROLLED past the games, rabbit race, rifle shoot and ring toss and the rides. Gavin stopped at the Tunnel of Love.

"I don't think so," April said, easing away from him.

"Too bad. You don't know what you're missing," he snickered, tugging her close to him again. She wondered what a trip through the Tunnel of Love with Gavin would bring. Her lips tingled at the memory of his kiss.

"And I don't intend to find out at the Farm Fair, either," she said.

The sweet smell of sugar and grease on top of cooking foods gave way to the familiar smells of farm animals, manure, and hay. April's stomach lurched for a moment as her nose adjusted. She made a face and Gavin laughed.

"City girl," he teased.

They stopped at an enclosure where a black and white pig lay on her side. Her massive body took up half the pen. Flies crawled around her ears as six little piglets sucked eagerly on their mother, pushing and shoving to secure a place and keep it.

"I didn't know pigs got to be so big. She's huge!"

"Don't call 'em pigs for nothing," Gavin said with a soft chuckle.

"Different colors, too. Aren't they all supposed to be pink?"

"Go tell that to the pig!"

Children and teens slopped their hogs, brushed them and sat on small stools outside their stalls.

Next were 4-H exhibits of giant vegetables and dioramas of solar heating ideas for farms and other energy-saving notions. Toward the rear of that section, against the back wall stood cages filled with rabbits. Huge lop-eared bunnies, with their ears hanging down, looked soft and cuddly in brown, black, white and mixed colors. Their cages lined the walls.

April crouched down to talk softly to each one. Only two children were tending their animals so she had a minute alone with each. The way their ears drooped down made them look sad. Tears pricked her eyes. She identified with the fluffy caged creatures. April held a breath, as she realized what was happening to her. Everything became clear in a flash as she saw the door close and lock on the cage of her future life in San Francisco. A sob caught in her throat.

She sensed Gavin watching her. Her smile melted into a frown and her brow knitted. A rustle behind told her he'd moved closer.

"What's wrong?" He placed his warm hand on her shoulder.

"I'm just like them."

"What?" Confusion clouded his handsome face.

"I'm like them. I'm living in a cage...or I will be," she said, standing up.

"What do you mean?"

"If I go back to San Francisco. I'll be walking into a cage and closing the door, forever. I'll be like one of these rabbits, a prisoner...a prisoner to what my father wants me to do...to be."

Gavin slipped his arm around her shoulder and she leaned into him. The realization of what her life could become shook April. She forgot where she was as tears burst through her frozen emotions and slipped down her face. Gavin turned her into his shoulder as she sobbed against his chest. He closed his arms around her and moved her slowly away from people and into a more private corner. April couldn't stop crying as he held her in silence. When she ran out of steam, she quieted down.

"I'm sorry," she said, embarrassed, reaching for tissues in her purse.

"Don't be." He wiped a tear from her cheek with his thumb.

"Maybe I'd better find Sunny and Mike," she said.

Gavin took her hand and guided her out of the exhibit and into the midway area. She found a bathroom and splashed cold water on her face. Standing by herself at the sink, loneliness engulfed her. She realized, no matter what else happened, there was no way she could go back to San Francisco. Although she didn't know where she'd go, her resolve not to return to San Francisco tightened in her gut and the decision chased away her sadness. She needed a different life. Becoming a rabbit in a cage wouldn't do. Not ever. Relieved, she returned to Gavin.

"I hate to see any animals in cages. I can't stand it," she said.

Gavin laced his fingers with hers and led her over to a quiet spot on the edge of the midway, behind the rifle shoot.

"Once my father brought home a parakeet. He used to visit it and coo to it for five minutes when he got home from work. But when he was at work, the poor bird jumped around the cage, trying to figure out how to escape and chattered as if he was looking for a mate. One day, I couldn't take it anymore. I took the cage outside and opened the door. The bird flew away. My father was furious and I was punished. But I didn't care. The bird was free and that made me happy."

Gavin squeezed her hand. "You should be free, like a beautiful bird, free to fly wherever you want."

She smiled at him. "I will be. Forever...free. You understand, don't' you?"

He nodded. "I think I do. Ready?"

She took a deep breath. "Ready."

Gavin led her to the last barn, which housed the cows. She saw Sunny sitting down and Mike talking with one of the owners.

She shot the firefighter an uncertain look. She'd exposed her personal feelings to him and counted on his keeping them to himself.

"Not going to say a word," he said, with a smile. "Our secret."

She smiled up into his eyes. Gavin turned and tugged April in the direction of some horses tied up at the end of the exhibit. He wandered over to pet one dark brown quarter horse. The friendly creature nuzzled him, suspecting he had food and Gavin pulled a small carrot out of his pocket. The animal took it and nudged him for more. He laughed and petted her while April watched from a distance.

"Horses are the best," he said, staring at the mare.

"She is beautiful. You love horses?"

He nodded. "I go riding through the back fields and down by Cedar Creek."

"By yourself?"

"You're not alone when you're with a horse." He patted the horse's flank after she nudged him again.

"I'm done here, let's go," Mike said.

Sunny looked at her watch.

"Do we still have time for a ride on the Tunnel of Love," he asked, taking her hand.

"We do."

"I know how you to hate to miss that ride, Sunny." He winked.

Sunny gave him a gentle smack with her hand but couldn't hide a smile. "Good try, Mike. We all know who wants to get me into the Tunnel of Love."

April wondered again if she wasn't missing something by not going on the ride with Gavin. As if reading her thoughts, he flashed her a wicked grin.

"It's not too late..."he started.

She gave him a friendly swipe on the arm and turned away to hide the pink in her cheeks.

AT DINNER ON SUNDAY night, Sunny offered her summer cabin to April.

"A cabin? That'd be wonderful! You two newlyweds could have your privacy back."

"You'd have your own place for a while...to get yourself together," Sunny said.

April put her hand over her eyes, pushing in her thumb to keep from crying, but it didn't work. She stifled a little sob and the tears leaked out. Mike gave Sunny a helpless look as his wife comforted the young woman with a hug.

"Why are you crying?"

"Because you're so kind...and you understand," April choked out.

"You can stay as long as you like. The community opens up tomorrow," Mike said.

"Could I move in then?"

"Sure," he said.

A knock interrupted the conversation. April went into the bathroom to wash her face and fix her makeup while Mike went to the door.

"Wanted to get a couple of things cleaned up in the spare room. Forgot to stow the paint can and clean the brushes before I left. I hope it's not too late," Gavin said as Mike stepped aside to let the young man in.

"Join us for dessert and coffee, Gavin?" Sunny asked.

"Sorry. Didn't know you weren't finished eating," he said.

Sunny set out a clean plate next to April while Mike filled another. She came out of the bathroom, surprised to see Gavin. He shot her a grin, held a chair out for her, then sat down. Sunny and Mike exchanged looks then smirked into their coffee mugs.

"I'm the dessert person. I made this. I call it Strawberry Surprise," Mike said, scooping out servings of the tempting-looking concoction into bowls.

"Am I going to be surprised if I like it?" Gavin joked, passing a bowl to April.

"Very funny. When was the last time you cooked, Fireman?" Mike retorted.

"No way I can compete with my aunt, Laura," Gavin responded.

"That's the truth! Christmas dinner at your house last year was amazing," Sunny said.

"April is moving into our cabin at The Birches," Mike said.

"She is?" Gavin gave her a sidelong glance.

"Tomorrow—wow! This is delicious, Mike. What's in it?" April asked.

"Can't tell you or it wouldn't be a surprise."

"You're going to live there...alone?" Gavin asked.

She nodded. "I certainly am."

"I can help you move," Gavin offered.

"I can handle it. She should have at least a running start before you move in on her," Mike said.

"What are you talking about?" Gavin asked.

"Don't play innocent with me, Gavin Dailey. You've been through every woman in Pine Grove, Oak Bend and probably most of Willow Falls already. Give her a little breathing room before you catch this doe in your headlights," Mike said.

Gavin's face colored.

"Is that true?" April asked.

"He's exaggerating...a lot! I've dated around, I admit it. But not *that* many girls."

"Then how many?" April asked.

"I don't know. I don't keep track," he responded defensively.

"Check the notches on his bedpost, April...on second thought, don't go up to his apartment to check...unless you want to become the next one," Mike joked.

"Not funny, Mike," Gavin flared.

"Apartment? I thought you live with your aunt and uncle?"

"I do. They converted the third floor of their house into an apartment for me."

"I see, so you do have a place for...all those women," she said, trying not to laugh.

"Not you, too! Sunny, a little help here?" he pleaded.

"You've come to the wrong place, Gavin. I'm afraid I have to agree with Mike." Sunny reached for the coffee pot and refilled their mugs. She licked a bit of Strawberry Surprise off her thumb, then kissed the top of Mike's head as she passed him on her way to the sink with the empty pot.

Gavin stood up. "I've got work to do," he said and marched into the spare room.

"Maybe we were a little hard on him," Sunny said.

"Does Barbara want you to send April home heartbroken and pregnant?" Mike asked.

"Mike!" Sunny put her hand on his arm to stop him.

"Gavin has been knocking up women?" April asked, aghast.

"He hasn't. I'm sorry, April. He hasn't...as far as I know. But he's a mover. Be forewarned," Mike said.

April finished her dessert, cleared the table and marched into the spare room to find Gavin finishing up. He tapped the top of the paint can with a hammer to seal it closed and wrapped the cleaned, wet brushes in paper towels before he noticed her in the doorway.

"Have you ever gotten anyone pregnant, Gavin?"

"What? Are you crazy? I have not," he said, giving the paint can a last pound with his fist

"That's a relief."

"Who told you I had?"

"Mike kind of suggested...well, I was about to cross you off," she said.

He got up close. "Don't do that," he said, softly, moving a lock of her hair off her face.

April looked into his blue eyes and melted under their heat. Sunny cleared her throat as she came into the spare room.

"I'm almost done here," Gavin said.

"I'd say," Sunny remarked, grinning.

April moved away. "I've got to pack."

He squeezed her hand before she drifted too far. "I'm serious about helping you tomorrow."

"Come by at eleven. We'll be ready about then," Sunny said.

He smiled "See you tomorrow." He tucked the paint brushes in a plastic bag before walking to his truck.

Sunny followed April into her room and flopped down on the bed. "Need help?"

April shook her head as she pulled clothes out of the dresser.

"Want to talk about him?" Sunny asked.

"Who?"

"Gavin—who else?"

April shook her head and continued folding her T-shirts.

"You're falling for him, I see it."

"I'm not. I don't even like him. He's...provincial...a farm boy," said April.

"He's no 'boy', April. Don't kid yourself. And I don't think he's provincial. I like Gavin. If he hadn't been so much younger...and Mike not here...who knows?" Sunny stared at April.

"You had a thing for Gavin?"

"He had a thing for me. Made Mike crazy. He still doesn't trust him."

"So that's why he's always hanging around here?"

Sunny laughed. "Are you blind, girl? He can't stay away from you."

"All he does is tease me and make me uncomfortable."

"That's how guys show you they like you."

"Brian didn't do that."

"Brian?"

"My boyfriend from grad school."

"Brian took off, didn't he?" Sunny asked.

"Off to Hong Kong. Didn't even look back."

"Do you miss him?"

"Not for a minute."

"I'll bet you miss Rusty, though."

"Sometimes...I do," she said, sitting down on the bed next to Sunny.

"Gavin is here. He's not going anywhere...and what a hunk!"

"Oh?"

"Don't tell me you haven't noticed? Every woman in the county knows who he is. Get real, April," Sunny said.

"So he's good looking..."

"You could do a lot worse."

"I already have!" April laughed.

THE NEXT MORNING AT eleven sharp, Gavin knocked on the door of the old Victorian. April let him in.

"Good morning, Springtime. Ready to roll?"

"Yep." She smiled and opened the door wider to let him in. His nickname for her was pleasing, sweet and affectionate.

"Where's your stuff?"

April pointed at the luggage and two boxes, then stepped aside.

Sunny entered, looking relieved. "Thanks for coming, Gavin. Mike has a horse emergency and we could never manage all this by ourselves."

"No problem, Sunny," he said, picking up several suitcases and carting them out to his truck.

April lifted one of the small boxes and followed.

Once her belongings were stowed, Gavin got behind the wheel and closed the door. The women followed in Sunny's car. When they got to The Birches, a mere mile away, Gavin carried everything down to the deck. Sunny sank into a chair.

"I'm beat and it's only eleven thirty. Must be coming down with a cold."

"Why don't you go on home...go back to bed. Gavin can help me, can't you?".

He nodded. "Sure."

Heaving a grateful sigh, Sunny got up and left.

Gavin hauled the valises and the boxes into the house. He hauled them here and there, under April's orders. Most of her possessions went into the larger bedroom. A queen bed, four-drawer dresser, a captain's chest at the foot of the bed, and small dressing table, all in oak, were the only furniture in the room. The two large windows had blue and white checked curtains. A rag rug of blues, greens and gold graced the floor between the bed and the dresser.

The small house was bright and cheerful, lifting April's spirits. Hope and happy anticipation filled her heart as she wandered from room to room. Returning to the bedroom, she instructed Gavin to lift one case onto the chest. She opened a drawer. The fireman stretched out on the bed. As she walked by to drop some tops into the dresser, he grabbed her wrist and pulled her down, trapping her underneath him.

"Springtime..." he muttered as he lowered his mouth over hers.

His slow, leisurely kiss started a fire inside her. She wound her arms around his neck as he braced himself, propped up on each elbow with his fingers in her hair. His lips pulled gently at hers until she opened. She sighed as his tongue teased hers. Her hands moved up into his hair as he deepened the kiss. The heat between them increased. April was lost in Gavin's embrace until a loud meow coming from the deck interrupted them. Opening her eyes, she gently pulled away from an unhappy Gavin and got up to investigate.

When she opened the front door, a lively, male, ginger striped cat bounded in. He wound around her legs, purring. Then he jumped up on the kitchen table. Laughing, April shooed him off and looked for something to feed him, but there was no food suitable for a cat in the refrigerator or the cupboard.

"Sorry, kitty. I'll put cat food at the top of the list when I go to the store."

She knelt down to pet him as Gavin came through the door, straightening out his shirt.

"Your cat?"

"Never seen him before," she said.

"Looks like he's adopted you," Gavin said, reaching down to scratch the animal behind his ears.

"I think I'll call him...hmmmm," she said, thinking, her gaze tipped up to the ceiling, her hand on her throat.

Then her focus narrowed on Gavin's face.

"Romeo!"

"That's *his* name, not mine," he huffed.

She chuckled and touched Gavin's face. He took her hand and kissed the palm.

"You need to get some food in the house. Come on. I'll take you," he said.

April climbed up into the truck again and they headed for the grocery store. Once again, Gavin proved helpful as they lugged the brown paper bags into the small house. As she unloaded, a meow came from the deck. April fished a small can of cat food out and put it in a bowl. She opened the screen door and Romeo made a beeline for the food.

"I've got to get to the stationhouse," he said, moving toward the door.

"Thanks for helping. I needed you."

"That's what I like to hear," he laughed, "I've got Sunday off. Want to go on a picnic?"

"I'd love to," she replied.

"Pick you up at noon," he said.

April left, followed closely by Romeo, to walk with Gavin to the parking lot. He pulled her to him. Resting her palms on his pecs, heat started inside her. He stooped for a quick kiss then drove off.

Chapter Five

In Allentown, Juan and Caleb walked into Googie's Diner. They sat in their favorite booth, waiting for the waitress.

"Ceci, remember that guy, the big guy we used to hang with?

"One with the red hair?"

"That's him."

"I remember him. Big tipper, cute, too. Couldn't get anywhere with him, though."

"He had a girlfriend, didn't he?"

"He lived with some chick."

"Know her name?" Juan asked.

Ceci shook her head. "He told me her name once, but I forgot. I was waiting for him to ask for my number."

"He didn't?" Caleb asked, his eyes looking her over.

"All hung up on that girl...whatever her name was...whadd'll it be today, boys?" she asked, raising her pen to her order pad.

AFTER UNPACKING HER groceries from a tiny market nearby, sweeping up, making the beds, April cooked a frozen dinner, then sat on the deck with a glass of wine. Most of the members of the community were due to arrive later in the month, so April was alone. She pulled out her diary, intending to write.

The sun was setting. She drank in the quiet of the early evening on the deck with only the chirp of bird songs to break the silence, when her cell started to sing. She looked at the display and couldn't believe her eyes as she read "Bear", her nickname for Rusty.

April stood and picked up the phone with shaking hands.

"Who is this?" she asked, her voice pumped up with anger hiding fear.

"It's me, Bear. Who did you think it was?" Rusty asked.

"Bear? You're dead. I saw you get blown up with my own eyes, so who is this?"

"It's me, Sugar Bear, honest."

April sank down hard on the bench at the table, dropped her hand with the phone in it to her side and stared into space. Sugar Bear is the name he called her.

"Sugar Bear, Sugar Bear!" Rusty called.

"Rusty, it's really you," she said and started to cry.

"Yes, darlin' it's me. Don't cry April. I'm okay. Nothing happened. I can't talk now. I'm coming to see you in a couple of weeks, but don't tell anyone, okay? Have to get some things straightened out here first. Text me directions, okay, baby?"

"Wait, wait. I want to talk to you. What happened?"

"Can't talk now, baby. See you in a couple."

The call ended.

April sat staring at her phone, not sure whether she'd actually talked to Rusty or dreamt it. She checked her latest calls and there it was, Rusty's number. He'd said not to tell anyone, but she needed to talk.

April walked the mile to Sunny and Mike's place, joining them on the back porch. Sunny was cuddled up in a blanket on the glider with her husband. Candles burned to spread light against the creeping darkness of night. April eased down on a chair, needing to open up about her phone conversation with Rusty.

"I'm not supposed to tell anyone, but I have to. I can't believe he sounded so casual. He was alive...all this time and he never called me, to check on me in the hospital or anything. I could have been dead and he wouldn't have known. And the grieving! He let me think he was dead all this time and I...and I...and..." April broke down, sobs wracking her body. Sunny scooped her into a hug, holding her tight as she struggled to gain control.

When April calmed down, Sunny asked, "What are you going to do?"

"I don't know. He said he's coming to see me, but I don't want to see him. How could I ever have planned to marry someone who was so...so callous?"

"What about Gavin?" Sunny asked.

"What about him?"

"He's stuck on you. Is Rusty coming here to get you back? Are you going off with Rusty again when he shows up?"

"I'm not going anywhere with him. He has a lot of explaining to do," April said. She glanced at her watch. "It's getting late. I'm going home. I've imposed on you enough."

"Hey, it's no imposition, April. You're family. Come on, I'll give you a ride," Mike said, rising to give her a hug and grab his car keys.

"You're nicer than family," April said. "At least my family."

April was jumpy, so Mike checked out the cabin to make sure it was safe before he left her.

She undressed, grabbed a book and went to bed. An hour after turning off the light, she tossed restlessly, unable to sleep. She looked out the skylight at the bright moon and tried to sort out her feelings.

Whether she liked it or not, she was still engaged to Rusty—at least until she told him otherwise. But she had developed feelings for Gavin, even if it was mostly a physical attraction. How was she going to handle this new road block to getting her life on track?

She knew she didn't have the whole story from Rusty yet, still, until she broke her engagement with him, she should keep her distance from Gavin. It was the only fair thing to do, even if she didn't like it. Emotional exhaustion finally set in and she fell asleep to the gentle meowing of Romeo from the back fence.

THE NEXT WEEK PASSED in a blur of activity in the community. People moved into their cabins for the summer. April helped out at The Birches and then with Sunny, who couldn't get her energy back. Gavin was occupied with emergencies and farm chores. She was glad he wasn't around much, making distance easier to maintain though she missed his easy smile and his soft lips.

April went to dinner at Sunny and Mike's house on a balmy Friday night in June. Mike was at the grill in the backyard with the dogs. Sunny smiled so broadly, April knew something was different.

"What's up with you?" She shot her friend a quizzical glance.

"I'm pregnant!" Sunny blurted out.

April screamed with joy and hugged her friend.

Mike beamed, too. "Don't I get any credit for this?" He asked.

"Congratulations, Mike. A mom! Sunny you're going to be a great mom," April said, jumping up and down, her face brightened by a huge grin.

"There's something else..."

"What?"

"You know I'm organizing the art auction for the A.S.P.C.A. again this year, right? Mike wants me to take it easy now that I'm pregnant. So, would you consider being my co-chair and helping with the event?"

"I'd love to. Something to do with myself instead of watching kids while people move in. Thank you, Sunny," April said without hesitation.

"I figure with your MBA, you might have ideas about how to increase the take."

After dinner, they planned a schedule of meetings. April walked home, preoccupied with her new project. She didn't see Gavin strolling toward her.

"Hi, Springtime," he said, twirling a sprig from a pine tree.

She looked up and smiled at him.

"Out alone after dark?"

"Is there some reason I shouldn't be?" She asked, a nervous frown on her face.

"Coyotes," he said, trying to hide a smile.

"Coyotes!" Immediately afraid, she moved closer to him.

"Don't worry, I'll walk you home." Gavin slipped his arm around her shoulders.

As they continued on in silence, she watched the moonlight play on the pine trees and cast shadows on the road.

"Sunny asked me to help her with the A.S.P.C.A. art auction," April said.

"You'll be here for a while, then?" He stopped and pulled her around to face him, lacing his fingers with hers.

"At least until the auction's over, the first of September."

"Then you're leaving?" He took her other hand in his, preventing her from turning away or walking on.

"Maybe. I don't know what my plans are. But staying to help Sunny is the least I can do after all she's done for me." April noticed his dark hair shining in the moonlight and reached up to touch it.

"Two more months..." He looked directly at her, as though trying to read her face in. He slipped one hand around her waist.

"By then I should know where I want to be." Sensing he was close enough to kiss her, April stepped back, pulling one hand from his grip.

"Any chance you'll want to be here?" He resumed their walk to her cabin.

"In this hick town? Doubtful."

"Sure made up your mind fast." He held on to her hand.

"I've been here a couple of weeks..." She swung their arms up and back.

"You think that's enough time to know people?" His sharp eyes studied her face.

"Maybe, maybe not." She shrugged but left her hand in his.

"Keep an open mind."

"Why? Why do you care if I like it here or not?" She turned to face him, challenge flashing in her eyes.

Silence greeted April's question. She looked up at the moon, waiting for an answer.

"We responded to three emergencies today," he said, changing the subject.

"Three? Sounds like a lot for this place."

"We cover Oak Bend and even Willow Falls if they need help."

"What happened?"

"One heart attack, one broken arm—kid fell out of a tree—and one asthma attack."

"Did you know what to do?" April stopped, dropped his hand and waited for his answer.

"I've taken first responder training. I'm not a paramedic, but I know what to look for and what to do until they arrive." He surrounded her hand with his larger one and continued walking.

"I didn't know that." She shifted her gaze to the moonlight shining on the stone. path.

"There's a lot about me you don't know." He pulled her closer.

"You have two months to show me everything there is to know about Gavin Dailey," April responded.

"Everything?" he snickered, raising an eyebrow.

He pulled her close to him in the shadow of a pine tree and kissed her. April was caught unaware but didn't struggle to get away. She let him deepen the kiss, softening against him, pushing thoughts of Rusty from her mind. Finally, as she felt her bones melt, Gavin broke the kiss and stepped back.

"You are beautiful in the moonlight," he said his gaze traveling over her hair, the red and gold highlights glimmering in the soft glow of the moon and down to her face, stopping at her lips.

"A kiss in the moonlight...sounds like a great title for a song," she said.

"Not just any kiss, April's kiss in the moonlight," he corrected.

He took her hand and they strolled down the path to her cabin, in no hurry to part.

The moon's brightness shone down on them. They walked along in silence, looking at the cabins, many already dark, some with tiny lights still shining in back bedrooms or upstairs lofts. The quiet blanketed the community, with most residents already asleep. As they approached the cabin, they heard the hungry howl of Romeo, who paced on the deck railing.

"Thanks for walking me home," April said, moving away from Gavin before he could kiss her again.

"I know a better way to thank me," he said, approaching her.

"You're right," she said, sticking out her hand. "Thank you."

Gavin laughed, took her hand and jerked her into his arms with one tug. He wound his arms around her and captured her lips with his again. She knew she should stop, but he was so tempting, she couldn't. *A few minutes...*

She broke away and looked up into his eyes. He smoothed her hair with his palm as she reached up to touch his face. His dark hair looked almost blue black in the moonlight, the two-day growth of beard shadowed his angular face making it even more attractive.

"Tomorrow's our picnic. You didn't forget, did you?" He asked.

She shook her head.

"I'll be here at noon. I have a surprise for you," he said, his eyes twinkling.

"Better be good, Fireman," she said, standing on the deck of her cottage.

"It is," he replied.

Gavin turned away from her to head back to the yellow house on the lake. April watched him amble down the path, wrestling with her emotions. Rusty. Gavin. Gavin. Rusty. There were too many feelings and not enough facts. Her gaze scanned the deck of the cabin across the way, the one belonging to Shirley and Hal Baron. She spied Hal sitting on his deck holding a ceramic mug.

"Hi there." Hal waved.

She smiled and waved back.

"Care to join me?" he asked.

"I have to feed Romeo. Why don't you come over?" she invited.

Hal descended the five steps to the lawn and joined her on her deck. He watched April dish out food to the hungry cat. Romeo wolfed it down, keeping his sharp eyes on April and Hal while he ate.

"Couldn't help but notice you and Gavin seem to be...getting along? Dating?"

"We're not dating."

"Could have fooled me. What do they call it now...hooking up?"

April blushed and shook her head. "We're definitely *not* hooking up!"

"Sorry, sorry. I'm out of the loop."

"Do you know what that even means, Hal?"

"Another term for dating?"

"It means sleeping together...we're *not* sleeping together!"

Hal blushed. "Geez, sorry. I didn't know it meant *that*. I apologize."

"Gavin and I are...friends. That's all." She looked up at the moon to avoid Hal's keen eyes, hoping he'd believe her...hoping she'd believe her own words, too.

"Too bad. He's quite a catch...a great guy. You know he saved Sunny's life two years ago?"

She stopped petting the cat, turning her attention to Hal.

"The cabin caught fire and Sunny passed out inside from the smoke. Gavin saved her, revived her and the dog, Trixie, too. He's a hero...brave guy." Hal sipped his coffee. "Don't know if I'd have the guts to do what he did...charge into a burning building."

"This cabin burned down with Sunny and Trixie in it?"

"Yep. All the way to the ground...nothing left."

"Did Sunny rebuild it?"

"Mike rebuilt it...for her."

"That's so romantic. Gavin saved her, huh?"

Hal nodded and took a sip of his coffee. "The kind of guy you can count on, April."

"Okay, Hal, you can stop selling Gavin. I'm...I'm...not available anyway, uh, not completely available right now."

He cocked a raised eyebrow at her. "You're seeing someone else?"

"It's complicated."

"I don't mean to pry. Time to hit the sack," he said, standing up.

April gave him a hug.

"Shirley and I are here if you need us," Hal said, giving April a pat on the back.

She smiled at him then went in to bed but sleep didn't come. She shrugged on a robe and padded out to the deck. Romeo was sitting on the railing, licking his paws and washing his face.

She pulled a chair over and sat next to him.

"What am I going to do, Romeo? Two guys. One is maybe a brave guy, a hero. The other is or was the love of my life, but now I don't know who he is. Who would you pick?"

The cat continued cleaning himself.

"You're no help. Just interested in doing your thing. And after feeding you." She made a face and sat back in the chair, her gaze scanning the sky and petting the animal. The tom purred, then licked her hand. She glanced at him and he stared back, as if trying to communicate.

"He's the one I should choose?" She looked at the cat again. "That's what I thought."

She kissed his head, then returned to the big bed, slid between the sheets and was asleep instantly.

Chapter Six

April shoved her legs in jeans and slipped a pink tank top over her head. She pulled her hair back into a ponytail. Small pink dangling earrings, a dash of make-up and sneakers completed the outfit. Gavin was right on time but April was still applying lipstick when he knocked on the door.

"Coming!" She called, putting the tube in the front pocket of her jeans. She slipped a comb in the back one and went to the door.

Gavin whistled a low whistle. "You sure do justice to a pair of jeans...ready?"

With a nod, she left the cottage. Romeo was sunning himself on the deck railing and gave a low meow to Gavin.

"She's mine now, buddy," Gavin murmured to the orange cat who jumped down and rubbed against April's legs.

"I'll be back in time for your dinner, Romeo. Don't worry," she said, while rubbing him behind the ears.

They got in the truck and April turned around to look behind her, then peered at Gavin.

"Where's the surprise?"

"Coming...Be patient, Springtime." He kept his left hand on the wheel, but laced the fingers of his right through hers.

April put his hand back on the steering wheel. "Two hands on the wheel, Fireman," she said.

They pulled up to a field surrounded by a split rail fence. A chestnut horse with a white blaze on her forehead grazed not far from the gate.

Gavin stopped the truck and retrieved a small picnic basket from the truck bed. April opened her door but didn't get out right away.

"We can't picnic here...there's a horse..."

"I know," Gavin said, putting two fingers in his mouth and whistling.

The horse picked up her head, and trotted over. April shrieked as the animal neared.

"Don't tell me you're afraid of horses?" he asked.

She took a step backward, keeping her eyes on the large, graceful creature.

"Nothing to be afraid of, City Girl," he said.

When the animal got close to the fence, Gavin reached over the wooden rail and patted her jaw. She nuzzled his hand affectionately.

"April meet Venus."

"Venus?"

"Laura named her 'cause she's a beauty. Silly name—picked by a woman, of course. Come closer. She won't bite you."

April inched closer until Gavin took her hand and yanked her over.

"Go on. Touch her. She's very friendly."

April put out a tentative hand, and the horse eyed her with huge, suspicious brown eyes, both mesmerizing and terrifying. Lifting a slightly shaky hand to touch the horse's forehead, April barely made contact when Venus whinnied and raised her head, blowing air from her nose. April gasped and jumped back. Gavin laughed out loud.

"You ladies will get used to each other. Venus is taking us to our picnic spot."

"How? There's no saddle or bridle on her. How is she going to take us anywhere?"

"We're riding bareback. It isn't far. Come on," Gavin said, picking up some ropes of nylon and leather slung over the fence. He unwound them to reveal a gray nylon harness with two brown leather leads attached to rings, one on each side. Venus stood still while Gavin fastened the harness on her head, keeping her eyes on April. Gavin hitched the horse to the fence, winding the leather leads around the rail, then guided April over.

"That's not a regular bridle, is it?"

"It's a harness. It's kinder. How would you like to have a metal bar behind your teeth all day?"

April made a face.

"Venus agrees with you. I don't want to use a bit...she's smart...doesn't need it, this works fine. Time for you to get on."

"What? How? I don't think..."

"Stop talking and listen. Climb up on the fence, then swing your leg over her."

"But there's nothing to hold on to?" She said, panic in her voice.

"Squeeze your legs a little tight and you'll be fine. I'll be right behind you."

April climbed up on the fence while Gavin held the horse. Holding her breath, she threw a leg over the horse's back but refused to let go of the fence post.

"You're gonna fall if you don't let go the fence. Let go, April!" hollered Gavin.

She did as he instructed and found herself square on the back of the horse, who turned her head to look at April, then back to look at Gavin. She gave a low whinny. April's hands were flat on the horse's back trying to get a grip.

Gavin tucked his hand through the handles of the picnic basket, threw a small blanket over the back of the horse, grabbed the reins and vaulted himself quickly and gracefully up and on behind April. He slid one arm around her middle and hugged her close to him, tightening his legs around Venus.

"Here. You hold this," he said, passing the picnic basket to April, who held onto his arm with a vise-like grip.

She shook her head.

"Take it, April."

She shook her head again, refusing to let go of his arm.

"I won't let you fall. Honest. I promise," he said, moving the basket slowly toward her.

April peeled the fingers of her right hand off his arm long enough to slip her arm through the basket then they gripped his arm again.

'You're cutting off my circulation...ease up."

She lightened her grip slightly, balancing the basket against her thigh.

"That's my girl," he said, clicking the reins.

"I'm *not* your girl!" She protested.

"I was talking to the horse," he lied. She knew it but she held her tongue.

April a let out the breath she was holding until Venus started to move, then she went back to panic mode. "We're moving! We're moving!"

"That's the whole idea. Venus is going to take us to a special picnic spot."

"Why can't we walk there?" She clutched his forearm stretched across her middle.

"Because this is more fun."

"For you, maybe..."

"Don't be such a city girl. Loosen up. Lean back against me and enjoy the ride."

Gradually April loosened her grip on Gavin's arm as the horse walked slowly through the field. April looked around, enjoying the view from so high up. She could see far-away houses and the splash of yellow from blooming forsythia almost a mile away. When she looked up, the sky seemed nearer. She leaned back against Gavin and relaxed.

"I ride like this all the time. Much better for everyone without the stupid saddle."

"You can't go fast like this, can you?" she asked, sudden panic seizing her brain.

"Venus likes to trot, but she won't be cantering today...most likely," he said, smiling to himself as April squirmed closer to him.

"Canter? That's like running, right?"

Gavin laughed and Venus stopped to look back at him.

"It's okay, girl," he said, leaning over April's shoulder to pat the horse's neck.

"It's like running. Relax, April. You're safe with me...and Venus, too. She's smart and gentle. She's Laura's horse, but I'm the only one who rides her."

Gavin moved the leads gently, steering the horse toward a secluded spot by Oak Bend Creek, a stream starting from Cedar Lake. The creek was about twelve feet wide with little rapids where stones jutted up above the surface. After a rainy early spring, the creek was high and running fast, bringing the sound of rushing water to their ears.

Wild flowers had bloomed and there were spots of color—lavender, pink, and yellow—scattered around the edges of the creek and in the field they crossed. The trees were still sporting the soft light spring green in their leaves. April marveled at the natural beauty of Gavin's special place. "Do you come here often?"

"Venus and I come here about once a week."

"Just the two of you?" She probed.

"What do you mean?"

"Do you bring other women here?"

"Not for a long time."

"But you did?"

"April, you're not the first woman in my life."

"But I am a woman in your life?"

"You're here, aren't you? What do you think?" He leaned in to whisper in her ear.

She didn't answer but straightened up, pulling away from him slightly. She let go long enough to touch the horse's silky shoulder, flattening her hand out. Venus stopped and turned her head to look at April and blew air through her nose.

"She likes you...and so do I," Gavin said, softly, nuzzling April's neck.

April leaned back against him again, closing her eyes for a moment. "Really?" She whispered.

"She bucked off the last girl I did this with," he said, as his lips grazed her neck.

April panicked and seized his arm with both hands.

"Relax! I was only kidding."

"Don't do that! I'm too new at this for...for...kidding."

He pulled her back against him and shook the leads gently to get Venus moving.

The horse continued walking, turning to the left, following the stream to a shadier section. She stopped when she got to a secluded, grassy clearing rimmed by pine trees on one side.

"This is it," said Gavin as the horse came to a stop.

"I bet you brought a lot of girls here. She knows exactly where to stop, doesn't she?"

Gavin colored. He took the picnic basket from her, bent over a bit and let it slide to the ground. Then he let go of her and dismounted.

"Where are you going? Don't leave me here like this?" She yelled.

"Hey, quiet down. You'll spook Venus."

"Spook her? What do you mean spook?"

"No loud noise. Here, lift your right leg over her shoulder, then slide down, I'll get you on this end," he said.

She shook her head.

"You're not coming down?"

She shook her head.

"April! Trust me! Come on, slide down to me," he insisted.

Her hands shaking, afraid to look down, she slowly moved her leg over the shoulders and neck of the horse. Venus shifted her weight and April squealed. Gavin put his finger to his lips and motioned her down. With both legs on the left side of the horse, she started to slide. Gavin grabbed her waist and pulled her to him. She slid down his body the rest of the way to the ground. His arms still around her, he stole a kiss before she was aware.

"That wasn't so hard, was it, Springtime?" he whispered, his voice caressing her.

April clung to him, her arms around his neck, trying to get her bearings. Gavin's hands pressed against her back, pushing her closer to him. She wanted to resist or thought she did, but the caress of the warm breeze on her cheek or was it his fingertips, brushing stray hairs out of her face, tickled her, excited her. His woodsy scent and hard body pushed any other thoughts out of her head. It was Gavin, only Gavin occupying her mind. He kissed her again. She parted her lips for his tongue and the embrace heated up.

In a minute, April came to her senses and pushed him away. He rested his hand on her cheek before she moved away. Venus walked to April and nudged her back to Gavin.

"I guess Venus thinks you're my woman, too," he said, taking the leads and looking for a place to tie up the horse.

He tossed the blanket to April who spread it out in the clearing.

"What do we have?" She asked, opening the basket and peeking inside.

"Aunt Laura's fried chicken and apple tart. Uncle Barney's potato salad, carrots and celery sticks and homemade lemonade," he said.

As he listed each item, April's stomach started to grumble.

"I guess riding affected your appetite," he said.

She flushed. "With a menu like that...wow!"

They opened the containers of food and made up plates. April spooned out the potato salad while Gavin loaded on chicken. He let

April give Venus half an apple he brought as a treat for her. The city girl ran her hand down the horse's forehead and muzzle. Venus muttered and stomped a foot. Gavin's smiled broadened as he watched his two best girls getting along.

"She's beautiful, Gavin. What kind of horse is she?"

"She's a quarter horse. The best kind. Fast, too." He said, picking up a chicken leg.

"Does she work on the farm?"

"Sometimes, though there isn't much for her to do. Laura grew up with horses. Barney bought Venus as a surprise anniversary present for Laura about five years ago. She used to ride her every day, but she sprained her ankle and gave it up. So I took over. She's more my horse now than Laura's...I take care of her, too."

"She likes you." April wiped some potato salad from her chin.

"She should, I'm the only one who gives her apples...except for to-day," he said.

April gathered up the dishes when they finished eating, saving their apple tarts for later. Gavin stretched out on the blanket, shading his eyes from the sun.

"Chickadees are out today," he said.

"You can tell...how?"

"Their song. It's distinctive. You can always tell when chickadees are around."

"I'm so ignorant."

"Here, listen. I'll show you...there...hear it? The chick-a-dee-dee-dee?"

He sat up.

April sat still, concentrating. "I think I heard it...there?"

"Right," he said, lying down again.

April rolled over on her stomach and propped herself up on her arms. She snapped off a long dandelion and inched closer to Gavin. He was on his back with his eyes closed to the sun.

She tickled his nose with the flower. He swatted at it and she moved it away quickly, only to move it back again. She did this three times, and then he opened his eyes and grabbed her wrist before she could get away.

"Teasing me? I wouldn't do that, if I were you," he said.

"Why not? An innocent tease..." she said, trying to hide her smile.

"No tease is innocent to me," he replied, desire lighting up in his eyes.

Her eyes widened and she moved back from him a bit.

"I'm kidding. What do you think I'd do? Take you right here on this blanket...against your will? Or maybe seduce you?"

She looked at Venus, avoiding Gavin's gaze. He reached over and took her chin in his hand, pulling her face around to be eye-to-eye with him.

"You don't think I'd do that, do you?"

"Would you?"

"Of course not. Why would you think that? I didn't bring you out here to—to take advantage of you...maybe we'd better go," he said, letting go of her chin and sitting up.

"No, no, Gavin. I don't think that," she said, putting her hand on his arm.

He looked at her.

"I don't. Honestly. I don't think that of you. Let's not leave; it's so beautiful here." She put her hand on his arm.

He lay back down on the blanket but the mood was broken.

"Why did you bring me here?" She asked.

"Why do you think? I wanted you to see this place. Want to get to know you a little better. Is that a crime?"

She inched closer, stretching out next to him on the blanket.

"Don't get too close now...I'm a dangerous man, you know," he said, rolling away.

"Don't say that," she said, putting her hand on his shoulder.

"It's what you think. Why are you so scared all the time, anyway?"

"My life is complicated. I have decisions and I don't...don't quite know what to do."

"A smart woman like you?" He rolled over to face her again. "Want to talk about it?" He asked, his fingers playing with the discarded dandelion.

She thought of Rusty and the last thing she wanted was to talk about Rusty with the man she was falling for. She sat up. "Let's talk about you. What do you want?"

"I want to live here. Build a house, have a family. This is a great place to raise kids."

"What about your folks? You're not from here, are you?"

"No, my mother died six years ago and my dad remarried. They live in Seattle and have a busy life of their own. Life is good here. Barney and Laura are my family."

"So you're looking for a wife?"

"I wouldn't put it like that...exactly..." A slight flush crept into his cheeks.

"What way would you put it? Oh, my...you're thinking about me for that—oh, no!" She said and stood up.

"Wait. You're jumping to conclusions here..." he lied, pushing to his feet.

April stalked over to the stream and found a stick. Crouching down, she dipped the end in the water, feeling the strength of the stream as the current pushed against it. Gavin came up behind her.

"Let's have those apple tarts," he said quietly, putting his hand on her shoulder.

April got up and joined him. They ate in silence. The perfect picnic hadn't turned out the way he'd thought it would.

"I don't want to live my life in a small town, Gavin. I thought I made that clear," she said as she packed up the plates and food containers.

"You don't know Pine Grove. Don't judge so fast," he said, stuffing garbage into a bag.

"You don't know me very well."

"Maybe not...but I like what I see—what I know, I mean," he said, blushing. He walked over to her and put his arm around her waist. April tried to pull away. "Come on, Springtime, only one hug."

"There is no such thing as only one hug with you, Gavin Dailey," she said, looking up into his eyes.

He leaned down and kissed her.

"I guess you're right. Maybe we should leave...while I still have control," he said, smiling gently.

Gavin helped April up on a tree stump and she mounted Venus from there. He got on behind her, securing her against him with his left arm and holding the leads with his right. Venus returned them to the field where the truck was parked and he drove April home.

They lingered on the deck with coffee.

"I enjoyed riding Venus. Maybe horses aren't so bad."

"Would you come for a ride again?"

She nodded and smiled at him.

He drained the last of his coffee and moved toward the steps. "Look out, April McKenna, country is getting under your skin."

She laughed and walked him to his truck.

Chapter Seven

April met with Sunny to brainstorm ideas for the art auction, and suggested selling advertising in the catalog and soliciting sponsorships from local businesses. Sunny wrote press releases and called artists, asking them to donate artwork. She tapped into her sources from her days as a top artist in New York City.

They divided the work into jobs to be done sitting at the phone or computer and those requiring activity, like visiting companies. April took the active ones and Sunny took the ones she could do sitting down.

Mike took April to buy a second-hand car from a man he knew to be reputable. The guy gave her a rock-bottom price and she shelled out most of the money she had saved living with Rusty. She needed wheels and now she'd be able to get around on her own.

After creating a schedule, April put on a turquoise suit and beige heels and visited the bank, a bread company, hardware store and the grocery store. She kept herself too busy to be available to spend much time with Gavin. She was rarely home when he called or stopped by because far away was the safest place. She found him irresistible.

Gavin had finished painting the spare room. Sunny had consulted April on where the crib and the dresser should be. She had pored over lists of baby names with April, laughing together at some of the funny combinations they had invented.

April watched Sunny and Mike, wishing she shared their kind of love with someone. She'd thought she and Rusty were in love, but she was never at one with him, like Sunny was with Mike. Maybe April had never loved Rusty enough, and perhaps he never loved her enough either. It was hard to take, but she wanted to face the truth. Rusty was fun but not a man to settle down with. Still, he was in her heart and she needed to know what had happened before she turned away.

What about Gavin? She was leery...he appeared to be a heart-breaker and her heart had recently been broken. Besides, their goals were different: she wanted travel, he wanted a home in Pine Grove, she wanted excitement, he wanted stability. He liked the sunrise, she favored moonlight. How could they ever get together, no matter how attractive she found him? She decided to focus on making the auction the best ever and forget about men for a while; perhaps easier to say than do.

One warm evening after finishing her dinner on the deck with Romeo and changing into shorts and a T-shirt, the fire siren went off. Shirley and Hal came out on their deck with binoculars. Hal looked around until he spotted the fire. April joined them.

"Where is it?" she asked.

"Looks like the barn at the Henderson place. Won't be long before we can smell the smoke," Hal said, watching the fire engine speeding along the empty road.

Shirley poured iced tea for them all as Hal watched the progress of the fire. After about fifteen minutes, they heard the scream of the volunteer ambulance siren and the rescue wagon pulled out of its house and sped toward the scene.

"That's unusual," Hal said.

"What?" April asked.

"Probably no people in a barn. But the rescue ambulance...must be for a fireman," Hal ventured.

April's eyes got wide. "A fireman?"

"Yep, ambulance is most likely for one of them."

"Gavin," she whispered. A chill went up her spine.

"My goodness, you've gone pale. Get in the car, April, I'll drive," said Shirley, jangling her keys. "You'll see. Everything'll be okay."

Shirley sped along the country road, pushing the speed limit. April's hand closed over the armrest with a vise-like grip. When Shirley stopped the car, April jumped out and raced over to the smoking barn. A fireman stepped in front of her. The ambulance personnel were taking out equipment.

"Sorry, Miss. You can't go in there," the firefighter said, releasing her.

"Who's injured?"

"Don't know. Two guys in there," the ambulance driver said.

"Who?" April asked.

"Gavin and Bobby, I think."

She gasped and tried to get closer. One fireman watching the barn from the outside held a walkie talkie to his mouth and was speaking to someone inside.

"Can you see him?" the fireman said.

Silence, as he listened to the response which sounded like static to April.

"Where?"

Again, static.

"Is he breathing?"

April's throat tightened and her pulse raced, pounding in her ears.

Again, static.

"Bring him out. Yeah. EMT's here," the fireman said and turned off the walkie talkie, "They're coming out."

The EMT's were ready. April's skin prickled with the tension in the air.

"They're coming, stand back."

Shirley joined April, who took the older woman's hand and squeezed it, then. Shirley put her arm around April's shoulder.

"Here they come," the fireman said, as a shadowy figure approached the barn door.

One man was carrying another. April strained her eyes but couldn't make out who was walking through the thick smoke. It wasn't long before she saw it was Gavin walking out with a limp Bobby slung over his shoulder. The EMT crew raced up as Gavin laid him down gently on the ground a safe distance from the barn. The rescuers went to work on the downed fireman immediately as he was unconscious. One worker gave Gavin a face mask attached to oxygen. Gavin coughed a few times and held the mask to his face.

"Gavin!" April shouted and waved before pushing past the other firefighters and running over to him.

He looked up at her and smiled. Before he could take more than a few breaths, she flew into his arms, tears spilling down her cheeks.

"Whoa, April! You're going to get full of smoke...what are you doing here?" He asked, folding his arms around her and smiling.

'Shirley and Hal told me—" She gasped for breath "...Told me the ambulance was probably for a fireman...and I thought it was you."

"It's okay, Springtime," he whispered, "I'm okay."

She closed her eyes, letting him hold her close, resting her cheek on his chest. When she calmed down and stepped back, she saw his eyes shining at her through his soot-streaked face.

"Your clothes may be ruined," he said.

She looked down to see smoke stains on her T-shirt and shorts.

"I don't care."

"You thought I was hurt, eh? Came running over here, for...a friend?" He asked, staring into her eyes.

She backed away and dropped her gaze.

"Because I don't want you to get hurt doesn't...*mean* anything."

He laughed. "Convince yourself, April, because you won't convince me," he said, draping his arm around her shoulders as he walked over to the captain.

"Good job, Gavin," the man said, clapping him on the shoulder and getting back on the fire truck.

Gavin got on the truck, too, while Bobby was whisked away in the ambulance. He waved to April as the truck pulled away. She returned to Shirley's car.

"Only friends?" Shirley said.

"Maybe a little more," admitted April watching as the fire truck disappeared.

"Maybe a lot more." Shirley laughed as she put the old car in gear.

Before bed, April said a little prayer of thanks for Gavin's safety. She denied any motive beyond concern for a firefighter. But her heart wasn't buying it.

On Sunday, Sunny called. "I need a favor."

"Anything!"

"My friend, Karen is visiting for a few weeks. She invited her cousin, Cassie. The problem is Cassie has to sleep on the sofa because with Karen, her parents, Ed and their baby there isn't enough room. Would you mind if Cassie slept in the spare bedroom at our cabin?"

"Of course not. That's fine. It'd be nice to have company at night, when coyotes howl."

"There are no coyotes here," Sunny scoffed.

"Gavin said there were."

"Probably to scare you into cuddling up," Sunny laughed.

Karen brought Cassie by. They thanked April and the new roommate placed her small suitcase in the smaller bedroom. She was a pretty young woman, younger than April, with a rounder figure, short light blonde hair and huge blue eyes.

When Gavin showed up, April and Cassie were drinking wine on the deck in the moonlight.

"Wanted to see if you needed anything...a lift to the store, maybe?"

"Thanks but that old junk heap I bought is working again," April said.

She made introductions, noticing Cassie's eyes light up when she looked at the firefighter.

"I have an early day tomorrow," April said to Gavin, hoping he'd take the hint and leave before she found herself in his arms again.

He turned to go. "Goodnight, April and Cassie...nice to meet you."

Cassie fairly glowed at him. "Same."

April headed inside to get ready for bed.

Cassie poked her head in the door. "You're not interested in that—that *hunk*?"

April hesitated a moment then shook her head silently.

"Do you mind if I make a play for him?" Cassie asked her.

"Go ahead. He's all yours." If he preferred Cassie then her problem resisting him would be solved, wouldn't it? She wasn't sure another woman was the best solution. Her heart rebelled. She regretted giving her new roommate the green light, but it was too late.

Cassie looked surprised but pleased.

"Actually, Cassie..." she began, then hesitated not knowing how to put her feelings for Gavin into words. She stopped and stood up.

April excused herself and went to bed before the truth slipped out of her mouth, making her true desires known to Cassie and to herself.

BREAKFAST CAME EARLY at the Dailey house. Laura set down bacon and eggs at seven fifteen. Gavin and Barney loaded their plates to fuel up for a full day of farming. Laura joined them.

"Haven't seen that pretty friend of yours around lately, Gavin."

"April? She's working on the auction."

"With Sunny?"

He nodded, his mouth full of food.

"Too busy to hang around you?"

"Laura..." Barney started, raising his hand.

"Just sayin'...haven't seen her. You two still...uh...friends?"

Gavin looked down at his plate, moving a piece of bacon around with his fork. He didn't want to hurt his aunt's feelings but he wasn't going to discuss April with her.

"Are we going to the auction, Laura?" Barney asked, changing the subject.

"I'll find out," Gavin volunteered.

"What's her name, anyway?"

"April. April McKenna."

"Will I be seeing her here for dinner any time soon? Just askin.'"

"Don't hold your breath," Gavin said.

"Guess she's not as smart as she looks," Laura sniffed and tucked into her food.

The men finished their breakfast, thanked Laura and headed out to the barn.

"You take the hogs, I'll handle the horses," Barney said.

Gavin agreed. He kept forgetting things and had to march back and forth from the barn to the trough to the barn again. He'd been preoccupied by April's cool attitude toward him all day. He was losing her and needed do something to win her back, but what?

First, he'd have to figure out why she pulled away in the first place. Grumpy and out of sorts, he stopped at April's before dinner and found both young women on the deck, where April was feeding Romeo.

"You ladies want to go for ice cream after dinner?" he asked.

Cassie jumped to her feet. "I'd love to. April?" She turned, giving April a pointed stare.

"I shouldn't eat ice cream. I'm getting fat." April focused her attention on the cat.

"Not from where I sit," Gavin said, moving his gaze over her figure, making April squirm.

"Do you mind if I go with Gavin?" Cassie asked.

April's head snapped up, she hesitated, then she shrugged her shoulders. "That's up to you, not me." Gavin wondered if she was indifference or honestly didn't care. And if she was…why? Her distance hurt far more than it angered him.

"Okay. I'll be back," he said, climbing into his truck.

When he knocked on the cabin door after dinner, it appeared that Cassie had convinced April to come along for ice cream, which suited Gavin perfectly. He held open the door of his truck, not expecting Cassie to hop in first, claiming the middle seat next to him. He caught the surprised look on April's face, He cocked an eyebrow at her, but she shrugged and looked away.

At The Creamery, he bought the ice cream and joined the women at a picnic table behind the store. Cassie was chatty and engaged him in conversation while April ate her cone quietly, listening. Cassie cozied up to him but April didn't do a thing to stop it. He flirtatious behavior caught him off guard.

He didn't like girls like her, obviously vying for his attention and ignoring her friend. She made jokes and smart remarks, prompting him to laugh despite his lack of respect for her. *Would April care if I liked Cassie?* When she inched closer to him on the bench, he didn't move away. Feeling the heat of April's gaze, he knew she didn't miss a word, a look or a gesture.

Desperate to regain his footing with April, Gavin seized on jealousy as his way to win her back. Though he didn't wish to hurt Cassie, he hoped April might get closer to him if he simply responded to the other woman's flirtations. Gavin moved closer to Cassie and put his arm around her shoulders when he finished his ice cream, and gave her his full attention. April coughed as though her ice cream slid down wrong. Halfway out of his seat to help her, Gavin pulled back, resisting the temptation to run to her side or get her water. He sat back down and forced himself to look at her without moving. Shame at ignoring her when she needed help filled his chest.

The coughing fit brought tears to April's eyes. Cassie hurried off to retrieve water and napkins. Gavin noticed even after she stopped coughing and wiped away the tears, new ones replace them when she saw Cassie move closer to Gavin. She put her hand over her eyes, trying to hide her response, but Gavin knew she was crying. Cassie seemed to be unaware.

"Coughing fits are the worst," Cassie said as she moved toward the truck, opening the front door.

April looked directly at Gavin as he approached the vehicle. She stared into his eyes. He recognized her hurt expression. Her eyes filled again as she silently slid in next to Cassie. The chatty girl rattled on and on about people he didn't know or care about—the whole way home. She appeared to be unaware of what was happening or that her silent audience had zoned out. When they got to the parking lot, April thanked Gavin without making eye contact and headed for the cabin.

"Want coffee, Gavin?" Cassie asked him.

He didn't reply but continued on down to April's deck.

"Coffee?" Cassie asked again.

Gavin shook his head, unable to stop watching April, who refused to make eye contact. He reached out for her arm but she yanked it away, tears brimming. Cassie, apparently oblivious to what was passing between Gavin and April, moved next to Gavin. He put his arm around her and she snuggled into his shoulder. April's lower lip trembled, she mumbled an excuse in an unsteady voice and pushed into the house. Gavin stood up. He knew she was crying because of him and he was ashamed, color heating his cheeks. Cassie took his arm and pulled him back.

"I think she's tired."

Gavin looked at her and making April jealous had backfired. Instead of wanting him more, April was hurt, and he was responsible. He needed to clear things up before leaving so he left Cassie on the deck and knocked on April's bedroom door.

"April...Springtime, please come out," he whispered.

"Go away, Gavin. I'm tired."

"Come on. Come on."

He was greeted by silence, then a click and glancing under the door, he noticed she had turned out the light. Feeling angry at himself and helpless, he made an excuse and returned home.

He avoided the main floor of the yellow house, taking the door leading right to his apartment instead. He took the steps two at a time. Once inside, he picked up his binoculars and headed for the window to stare at the stars. But searching for The Big Dipper didn't cut it. He grew restless. Had he ruined everything with April by being a jerk? Fear and sadness mixed with anger at himself. His heart had squeezed when he had sensed her distance. Seeing her expression of pain that he caused stabbed his guts.

He turned out the light and got into bed. Staring through the skylight, he noticed the moon was full.

"Traitor," he mumbled at the planet, blaming it for screwing up his life.

A day of physical labor had tired him. He drifted of, determined not to give up April and that he'd find the way to fixed what he had messed up, in the morning. His mother had often reminded him that the next day life would look brighter and he'd know how to solve his problems, then.

At breakfast, Gavin was surly and quiet. Laura served a stack of flapjacks and sat down.

"How was your ice cream double date last night?" she asked.

Gavin glared at her but managed to keep his mouth shut.

"What? It's an innocent question," she protested.

Gavin stuffed food in his mouth to keep from saying something he'd regret.

Barney cleared his throat. "Gavin, I've been having trouble with the mare we got last week. Do you think you could come out to the barn with me after breakfast?"

"Sure." Gavin nodded, grateful for something to take his mind off April.

"You're in some mood this morning, son. That young woman do something to you?" Laura asked.

"Won't talk about April," he said shortly.

"Well." Laura snapped back as if she had been slapped. "Guess I know when to shut up."

Gavin shook his head. "I'm sorry, Aunt Laura. It's not you."

They finished the rest of the meal in silence. Gavin and Barney left Laura in the house to clean up the kitchen.

On their way to the barn, his uncle broached the real subject of his trip to the barn with his nephew. Once they were in the barn and out of earshot of Laura, Barney faced Gavin. "Okay, what's going on?"

"I did something stupid last night," Gavin said.

"Yeah? You and a thousand other guys. What did you do?"

"A cousin of Karen's is staying with April for a few weeks and I...I used her to make April jealous." Gavin stuffed his hands in his pockets and slowed his pace.

"How'd you do that?"

"Put my arm around her, flirted with her, ignored April..."

"Stupid is right. What did you do that for?" Barney stopped and put his hands on his hips, looking sideways at Gavin.

"April was ignoring me, cooling off, I could tell. I thought she'd make a play for me."

"For a smart guy, you're pretty dumb. What happened?"

"I hurt her. She was crying, trying not to, but I could tell. Then she disappeared into her room and wouldn't come out." Gavin kicked at some small rocks.

"Go and apologize to her."

"Now?" Gavin looked up at his uncle.

"Now," Barney said, yanking the barn door open and motioning for Gavin to leave.

Chapter Eight

Gavin drove to The Birches, arriving a few minutes before eight, about the time people were getting up. Hal waved to him as the firefighter walked down to April's cabin. It was quiet until he heard the creak of the screen door. April came out wearing a short bathrobe and carrying a cup of coffee. She stopped when she saw him.

"Cassie is still sleeping," she said, casting her eyes down but not before he saw they were filled with pain.

"I'm here to see you."

"Why? You've moved on. You made that clear last night."

"April, please. I need to talk with you...alone. Can we go somewhere?" April motioned to him and walked down the stairs to the lawn. He followed her off the deck. They wandered down to the benches in a field near the tennis court. April sat down first, Gavin next to her. He turned to face her.

"I owe you an apology," he said, looking down and fidgeting with his keys.

"Why?"

"I was mean to you last night...on purpose."

April cast her gaze to her hands, her eyes filling with tears. She took a ragged breath.

"I was stupid. I tried to make you jealous. I hurt you instead. I'm sorry."

April raised her gaze to his. She brushed at the tears with her hand. Gavin caught one halfway down her cheek and wiped it gently with his thumb.

"I'm not interested in Cassie. Only you. Do you forgive me?"

"I'll think about it."

"Maybe this will convince you."

Gavin put his hand behind her head and eased her forward until he could kiss her.

She stared into his eyes. "Why were you trying to make me jealous?"

"Why have you been distant with me?" He countered.

April blushed. "It's complicated. I have a previous commitment, sort of...I can't explain it now. You'll have to trust me. Until I get this situation unraveled, I have to be noncommittal."

"After whatever this is gets resolved? Then?"

"I don't know. I can't say now." She looked away, picking at a thread on her robe.

He didn't get the answer he wanted. "Are you interested in seeing me?" he asked her pointblank.

"I...well...if...I...sort of...if I'm free," she stammered, red creeping up her neck.

"That's not good enough. Yes or no." He put his hands on her shoulders and gently but firmly turned her to face him.

"If I'm free...when I'm free...then...yes," she said, squirming to get loose from his grasp.

"You're not free? I thought the guy you were engaged to was killed."

"I thought so, too." She pulled her robe tighter around her when he dropped his hands.

"He's alive?" Gavin asked, rising up from the bench.

"Shhh. No one is supposed to know." April pulled him back down.

"So you're still engaged? Where is he?"

"I don't know where he is. I guess I am still engaged until I tell him we're not."

"You're going to break up with him, right? Why didn't you tell him when you found out he's alive?" Gavin pulled her chin up so her eyes were level with his.

"I was in shock and he was only on the phone for a few seconds." Her eyes remained steady, her body still.

"How are you going to end it with him if you don't know where he is?"

"He's coming to see me." April dropped her gaze and rubbed her palms together.

"When?" Gavin said, his brows furrowed his eyes cloudy.

"I don't know," she said.

"This is too crazy for me, April," he said, standing up to leave.

"I know it's a little...unusual," she said, pulling on his arm, "please don't decide anything until I know more."

"What if you stay with him...he moves up here?" He pulled her closer to him.

"That'll never happen." She whispered.

"How can you be sure?" Gavin demanded.

"Because I don't love him," she confessed, then lowered her lashes.

"Then you do want to end it with him?" He crossed his arms.

"Of course. Would I tell you about him if I didn't?" She placed her hand on his forearm.

Gavin looked at her in silence.

"What about me?" He gripped her upper arms with his hands, forcing her to look at him. She blushed.

"Look at me!" he commanded.

"I...I like you. Not sure about staying here. I want to see the world."

"See it with me." He said softly, pulling her up close, their lips a breath away.

"How? You're locked in here." April moved back but her eyes were still focused on his lips.

He pulled her to him roughly and kissed her hard on the mouth, possessing her. She whimpered and went soft against him.

"I want you, April," Gavin breathed in her ear, "and I'm not giving up."

She moved closer to him and he kissed her again, longer. She returned his ardor, their tongues dancing. They broke when they heard a cough. April looked over to see a foursome approach the tennis court.

"Get a room, Gavin," called out one of the young players.

"Shut up, Tom," the embarrassed firefighter called back, standing up, holding his hand out for April.

They returned to the cabin, where Gavin kissed her goodbye and drove off, watching her in the rear view mirror.

USING MOST OF THE REMAINING money she'd saved from her life with Rusty, April bought a dark pink suit for her meeting with the bank. Rusty had made enough to pay for their living expenses, so April had kept the money she had earned consulting for non-profit companies in Allentown. Rusty had been content to pay the bills and come home to a beautiful woman and a warm meal every night. A local bank had hired April part-time. She had been happy working and acting like Rusty's wife. He had been sweet with her, warm, loving, and generous.

But she hadn't loved him, not enough. She knew it now. So, did she love Gavin? She only wished she knew the answer. In the meantime, April had work to do, so she put Gavin out of her mind. For a while, anyway.

The meeting with Pine Grove National Bank went well. They agreed to become a sponsor, giving the A.S.P.C.A. twenty-five hundred dollars to use for promotion and advertising. April returned to the cabin hoping Cassie would be there to celebrate with her. April walked down from the parking lot, her spiked heels sinking into the soft ground, her business-like white blouse unbuttoned several buttons for comfort, her jacket slung over her shoulder.

"Cassie!" she called as she neared the cabin.

Instead of Cassie, Gavin came out, followed by a young man she didn't know and then Cassie.

"Who is this?" She asked Gavin.

"Meet Justin Barner, Deputy Sheriff. Justin, April McKenna."

April shook Justin's hand

"We're here to take you ladies out to dinner," Gavin said, his own gaze zeroing in on the cleavage revealed by April's blouse.

Cassie came out of the cabin dressed to kill in a low-cut light blue sundress, stealing Justin's attention immediately. April relaxed. Apparently, Justin was meant for Cassie.

When she realized Gavin was staring, April fastened the lowest button on her blouse and then laced her fingers with his.

"Great idea! I got a twenty-five hundred dollar grant from the bank for the auction today...a reason to celebrate!" she announced.

On their way to the parking lot, they passed Hal, on his knees weeding in front of his cabin. He stood up and pulled April aside.

"Don't tell me you're not dating. Shirley and I saw your demonstration...demonstration of...of, sucking face? Isn't that what they call it? This morning," Hal chuckled.

April laughed and blushed, quickly rejoining Gavin and the others. Gavin raised his eyebrows.

"Apparently our bench this morning wasn't as private as I thought," April explained.

They all piled into Justin's car and headed for the fried chicken restaurant...best fried chicken in the county, next to Laura Dailey's. Cassie put her arm through Justin's as they walked in. He couldn't take his eyes off her, pulling out her chair and hanging on her every word. Gavin and April tried not to laugh as they watched them get cozy. He moved closer to her and draped his arm around the back of her chair, resting his hand on her shoulder.

After dinner, Justin and Cassie went for a walk in the moonlight, while Gavin and April waited on the deck for Romeo to stop by for his evening meal.

"There's a chicken barbecue to raise money for the ambulance corps next Saturday. Will you go with me?"

"What's a chicken barbecue?"

"They cook up chicken and corn on the grill. People pay for the food and the profit goes to the volunteer ambulance service. They set up picnic tables and everybody comes. So?"

"A country thing, right?"

"I doubt they do this in Paris or Hong Kong, April," he said, laughing.

"Very funny! Okay. I'll go, I want to see what farm boys around here do with their free time," she teased.

"Farm boys! I warned you," he said, grabbing her around the middle and tickling her.

They struggled for a while, April shrieking and laughing at the same time. Hal and Shirley came out on their deck, concerned about the screaming until they looked over at April. They smiled and went back inside. She continued to struggle, knocking Gavin off balance. He let go of her to keep them from falling. She stepped back, panting. Both of them worked to catch their breath. The moonlight painted a warm glow on their faces as they eyed each other. He snaked his arm around her waist and pulled her to him. April tried to push away but Gavin gripped her firmly and wasn't going to let go. His lips met hers before they heard Cassie giggling. The couple parted.

Justin and Cassie were howling with laughter as they returned. His arm was around her shoulders with hers around his waist. Cassie's lipstick was smudged on Justin's mouth and cheek leaving none on her lips. They appeared to be drunk, although no one was drinking.

"Interrupting something...I hope," Justin snickered, laughing.

April blushed and turned away from Gavin as a loud meow preceded Romeo's appearance. She petted him then scooted into the kitchen to get his food, relieved to get away from the charged atmosphere on the deck.

The moonlight reflected off Justin and Cassie's heads, giving them the appearance of glowing. Cassie stayed close to him while his gaze met hers and fire between them ignited.

"Don't let me stop you," Gavin muttered, taking a seat near Romeo.

Justin blushed and turned away from the tempting young woman, took her hand and sat down. April returned with a bowl of cat chow and Gavin bid her farewell. Because, the men were expected to report to work early the following morning, they left. Cassie made tea and brought it on the deck. The women sat drinking, looking up at the moon.

"Moonlight is brighter in Pine Grove than anywhere I've ever been before," Cassie observed.

"You like Justin?"

"He's a hunk! Why didn't you tell me the truth about you and Gavin? I feel bad about...you know...I kinda flirted with him, when I didn't know he was yours."

"He's not mine."

"There you go again. Give it up, April. That guy is yours for the asking."

April turned her heated face away from Cassie and sipped her tea.

"Have it your way. I'm going to bed...planning to dream sexy dreams about Justin. I *love* men in uniform," Cassie gushed, getting up to go inside.

THE CHICKEN BARBECUE drew folks from all over the county. People knew they might someday need the ambulance service, so they all turned out to support the cause. Gavin and Justin arrived together to take April and Cassie. April wore a short denim skirt and two layered tank tops in shades of aqua. Cassie wore a low cut sundress in lavender. Justin reached for the deck railing, missed, and almost fell over when Cassie exited the cabin. His gaze roved over her ample curves and a wicked smile spread across his face.

They piled into Barney's car, which Gavin had borrowed in exchange for his truck.

"How long you planning to stay?" Gavin asked Cassie.

"Just a couple of weeks. I'm leaving for Europe soon."

"Europe?" Justin said, crestfallen.

"Graduation present. I'm going for ten days. But I'll be back."

"Back here?" Justin asked.

"I don't know yet. Should I come back here?" she asked, looking into his eyes.

There was silence from the back seat, then giggling. April was too embarrassed to look.

At the chicken barbecue, April ran into everyone she knew, Sunny and Mike, the guys in the band and people from The Birches. Sandy Gifford, the president of the bank was there, too.

"April! Howdy. Come meet Matt Daniels. He's the president of the chamber of commerce."

April shook hands with a tall, broad man, with thick white hair and a big handshake.

"You're in charge of the art auction, eh? We should meet. I'd like to tie in some chamber of commerce promotions with the auction."

April grabbed her purse and pulled out her calendar to schedule a meeting. One of the local hotel owners was there, too. She negotiated a special rate for participating artists while waiting in line for food.

The school principal showed up looking for April to talk about fund-raising for sports uniforms at the auction. It seemed everyone in the county knew about the auction and April McKenna being co-chair.

Laura Dailey made a plate for the young woman, since she was pulled aside repeatedly to make plans for the auction.

The local towns wanted to participate and benefit from the influx of visitors for the two-day event. Suddenly, auction co-chair was a full-time job. April took notes and listened to her stomach growl.

Gavin sat down with Justin and Cassie. Shirley and Hal joined them, along with Sunny and Mike and Karen and Ed and their little girl. April pulled herself away from the bowling alley owner to eat the plate Gavin handed her, and answer questions from her friends.

"So glad you're in this with me, April," Sunny said.

"That makes one of us! Not sure I'm ready for this," April said.

"Just a sleepy little town, April. What's the big deal," Gavin said, raising an eyebrow.

She made a face at him and dug into her meal. "Who made up this plate for me?"

"My aunt Laura. If you don't get in early, everything'll be gone."
April smiled.

"Looks like you've got all the contacts you'll need to blast this thing out of the water," Sunny said.

"I think so. I have a few ideas I want to bounce off Matt Daniels. Maybe he can organize the small businesses so I don't have to visit each one."

Before she could finish eating, some of the tables were moved away and Electricity got up to play. As people danced to Mike's singing, Al watched April closely and smiled.

With her seat taken away, she had to finish standing up.

"That's not good for your digestion," Laura Dailey said.

She turned around to face Laura. "Thank you so much, Mrs. Dailey, for making me a plate."

"Call me Laura. Can't let the young woman who's organizing this big to-do go hungry, can I?" she said with a gleam in her eye.

April blushed under Laura's frank scrutiny. The band began playing "I Can't Smile Without You." Gavin joined April and his aunt. He handed April's plate to Laura without taking his eyes off the young woman.

"May I have this dance?"

April extended her hand, he pulled her into his arms.

Her face flushed with excitement. "I can't believe there are so many people who want to get involved in the auction. I'll never be able to meet with them all in time. I've got to find a printer for the catalog, find a place to store the art, advertise, start selling tickets. It's already July Fourth. I'll never make it!"

"Slow down, April. Slow down. It'll get done." he said, pulling her closer.

She rested her head on his shoulder while ideas whirled through her mind. She sighed, happy for the first time since she could remember. Gavin's fingers played with her hair as he moved her slowly around the blacktop. They continued to dance even after the band took a break and recorded music began to play. Gavin didn't let her go, and April was content to stay in his embrace until there was a tap on his shoulder. Gavin didn't look pleased to see the other man trying to cut in.

"Give, Gavin. You've kept her all to yourself," Al said, taking April's hand.

Gavin had no choice but to give her over to Al. who was a little rough, stepping on her feet once or twice. Before he could get through one dance, Doobie cut in.

"Thought I'd save you from Al," he said.

April didn't believe him for a second. But he was a better dancer than Al, so she was happy, until Jack cut in.

"Thought I'd rescue you from Doobie. He's a lousy dancer," Jack said.

April laughed even though her feet were getting sore, as none of the band members could dance well. When Mike called everyone back and they started playing live music again, she was relieved. April found a seat near Sunny and sank down into the chair.

"I spoke with your mom today," Sunny said.

April looked up sharply.

"Do you give regular reports? You didn't tell them about Rusty, did you?"

"Of course not. A confidence is a confidence. But you mother said your dad insisted on coming to the auction."

"They're coming?"

Sunny nodded, a sympathetic expression crossing her face.

"Oh no," said April, resting her forehead in her hand.

"Barbara didn't argue with him. She's desperate to see you."

"This isn't good. He's coming here to take me home, not to support the auction."

"You're twenty-six years old, April. He can't take you anywhere."

"I have no income, no job, no prospects. He'll support me...if I go back."

"Maybe you can find a job?"

"Where? Here? How? When? I'm going to be incredibly busy the next six weeks."

Sunny squeezed her hand. Tears pricked at the back of April's eyes. Her father's

arrival would mean the end of her independence. Before she knew it, she'd be slammed into the internship, doing what he said, just like the rabbits in the cages at the Farmer's Fair.

Frustration, anger, and sadness welled up in her chest. She decided to go back to the

cabin alone. April set out on the road, walking slowly toward The Birches. Tears spilled down her cheeks as she watched her hard won independence fade away. Then her cell rang. She check the screen, a text from "Bear". She opened it.

See you Saturday.

She wasn't looking forward to a confrontation with Rusty but she needed answers to

the questions on her mind for weeks. She wanted to finish things with him so she could make room in her heart for Gavin. While she wouldn't admit to anyone else that she cared for him, she could no longer hide it from herself. She had fallen for him.

His persistence made it harder for her to deny. But she was still engaged to Rusty, so it was a good thing he was coming to see her soon. At least one thing in her life would be fixed, wouldn't it?

Chapter Nine

April was so busy organizing the auction, the week passed in a blur. Before long, Cassie was packing to catch her plane bound for Europe. She was teary-eyed at the thought of leaving Justin, who had spent every evening with her. April was going to miss her. Her presence helped her keep Gavin at a distance.

Wednesday night the young women barbecued for Justin and Gavin. With wine, beer and steaks, it was a festive occasion. They put music on and danced. April invited Hal and Shirley over to share the cake they got for Cassie. Hal brought ballroom music and they got in the groove. Shirley and Hal glided over the grass with precision and grace. The others sat on benches, watching, while the older couple tangoed across the deck.

As the moon rose, the men prepared to return home. They faced early morning work obligations. Justin took Cassie for a walk while Gavin stayed behind to help April clean up. Shirley and Hal went back to their cabin across the path.

"What's up with Justin and Cassie? Is he serious about her?" April asked, propping the door open so they could move in and out with ease.

"Don't ask me. I'm always the last one to figure these things out." Gavin dropped the mustard, salt and pepper on the kitchen counter and returned to the deck to retrieve dirty dishes.

"Come on, Gavin. Give." April stopped in the doorway, her hands on her hips.

He laughed. "Why do you think I know anything?"

"He's your best friend. Guys talk. Come on," April coaxed.

"He likes her," Gavin said, balancing a pile of plates in his arms.

"Duh! Come on," April said, following him inside.

"I can't, April. You'll tell Cassie, then I'm in trouble."

"I won't. I promise."

He shook his head. "He's my best friend!" Then he returned to the deck and picked up a large oval platter.

"Okay, okay!" She said, holding up her hand. April wiped off the table and returned to the cabin, tossing the dirty sponge in the sink. After they put away the last dish, Gavin moved closer to her, pulling her into his arms. He buried his face in her neck, while his lips caressed her soft skin. She moved back away from him.

"Rusty's coming to see me on Saturday," she tossed out.

"What?" Gavin stiffened.

"He's coming here but no one's supposed to know." April chewed her lip as he released her from his embrace.

"I'm confused."

"I'll have the facts soon...and I can break my engagement to him then and be free..." she said, avoiding his stare.

"That's why you've been avoiding me?"

She bit down on a hangnail, blinking rapidly as she nodded.

"Who would think you were engaged to a dead man?" Gavin said, shaking his head.

She crossed the room to the cabin door but he grabbed her wrist and held her on the spot. "Is he more important than I am?"

"It's not a contest, Gavin. Until I know what's going on..."

"All right, then. How long is he staying?" Gavin asked, nervously shifting his weight from foot to foot.

"One night...I think. He didn't say." April's gaze searched for Romeo, hoping the cat would provide an escape from this subject.

"One night...in your bed?" Gavin asked his brows knitted over angry eyes, his hands tightening on her upper arms.

"I'm not planning to sleep with him."

"Not *planning* to?"

"I'm not *going* to sleep with him," she said, her face flushing.

"You've slept with him before. Why should I believe you won't now?" He asked, dropping his hands from her arms, his eyes still angry.

"Isn't my word good enough?"

"You were engaged to him...found him irresistible, right? Now you say you don't anymore—just like that? Do you take me for a fool?" Gavin turned away.

"I'm asking you to believe me. I don't love Rusty anymore." April closed her hand on his forearm.

"We'll see," he said, ripping his arm from her grasp and storming down the steps.

"Gavin," she called after him but he didn't turn around.

He kicked a bunch of rocks out of his way as he strode up the path to the parking lot, jumped into his truck and hit the accelerator. April stood on the deck watching him drive away until she heard a loud meow behind her.

"Great! Where were you when I needed you?" She asked the cat before she went into the house to get his food.

LONELINESS SWIRLED around April after Cassie's bus pulled out. She'd grown used to having the other girl around, and things were too quiet without her bubbly personality. Only one day remained before Rusty's arrival. Gavin stayed away. She missed him, though she wouldn't admit it. He'd made a place for himself in her life without her realizing it.

She opened her pocket calendar and focused on the auction because she didn't want to think about Gavin or Rusty, or what she might find out when Rusty arrived. Life was complicated enough.

By noon, she was restless and went for a walk. She found herself approaching the field where Venus had been waiting for her and Gavin on their picnic date. April walked down to the split rail gate and spied the horse grazing about fifty feet away.

"Venus!" she called, waving to the mare.

The horse raised her head and trotted over. She wore a harness and one lead but no saddle. The second lead was hanging carelessly over the gate. April fastened it to the harness and guided the horse closer to her. She petted the large head, especially the white blaze, which fascinated her.

"What are you doing out here all alone?"

Venus stared at her and snorted, making April laugh. She picked some succulent grass from her side of the fence and offered it to the horse, who scooped it into her mouth with her soft lips.

"So the grass *is* greener on the other side, eh?" She asked the horse.

Venus snorted again and stomped one foot until April picked more grass. She continued to pick grass, and feed the mare while she talked. Occasionally, she stroked the horse's soft muzzle. Emboldened by the sweet-natured horse, she tied Venus up as Gavin had done, and straddled the fence, then climbed up. She looked around, didn't see anyone, and mounted the horse.

April didn't see Gavin. She struggled to untie the lead slung around the fence while hanging on to the mare's neck.

"He did this. It didn't *look* hard."

She slipped every time she reached out.

"Hey! Venus!" Gavin called.

The horse looked up and whinnied. April panicked, throwing her arms around the mare's neck. Gavin strolled down to the fence. He climbed up, mounted Venus and untied the lead from the rail.

"Let's go," he said, making a clicking noise with his tongue as he slipped his arm around April's waist.

The horse began trotting immediately, then broke into a canter as she neared the woods. The wind cooled April's skin as they flew past trees. He gripped her firmly about the waist and she tightened her thighs.

She moved her body to the rhythm of the horse and Gavin. The three of them became one. April no longer feared the horse. The speed at which they rode through the field was exhilarating. But as Venus neared the woods, she slowed to a trot and then a walk.

Gavin led them along his favorite trail. The easy silence between them was broken only by the steady scuffle of Venus's footfalls and the subtle song of a chickadee. Shafts of sunlight penetrated the forest where there was a break in the trees. April shivered as they rode through the shade. Gavin pulled her back into his chest where the heat from his body would warm her. She relaxed, undulating easily with each step Venus took. April loosened her grip on Gavin's arm and he flexed his fingers. A small smile broke out on her face as April filled her lungs with fresh air and the scent of the horse mixed with Gavin's pine soap in her nostrils.

"You've got a good seat, there," he said.

"I beg your pardon?" April craned her neck, trying to have eye contact.

"Means you sit a horse well, April. I'm not commenting on your butt...though it looks pretty good, too," he said and then laughed.

"I've got a lot to learn," she chuckled.

"You can say that again!"

She elbowed him in the ribs and laughed.

"Don't you dare tickle me or we'll both go sliding off!" she wailed.

After their last encounter, she figured he'd distance himself from her but the way he held her to his body convinced her otherwise. He leaned down and let his lips brush her neck softly.

"Springtime," he whispered.

"What? What did you say?"

"Nothing," he replied. But she'd heard him.

Venus didn't tire easily and their ride continued through the sun-dappled woods and out onto the back fields of the Dailey farm and across to the Smythe place, down to Smythe Pond. Venus walked over to the pond and dipped her head for a drink.

They soaked up the sun for a bit, heat building up in her veins. The cool, calm water of the pond invited her to jump in and cool off. They dismounted.

"If you weren't such a prude, we could have a nice skinny dip in the pond," he said.

"What makes you think I'm a prude?" April cocked an eyebrow at him.

"You telling me you'd take your clothes off and jump in the pond with me?"

"Maybe not...but not doing it doesn't make me a prude," she said, chewing her lip.

"If it doesn't then I don't know what does. It's hotter than blazes in the sun. I'd love to go for a swim. You game?" A gleam of desire lit up in his eyes.

"I thought you weren't talking to me." April stated, changing the subject.

"I thought you were afraid of horses," He shot back.

"Other horses...maybe. But not Venus."

"Haven't answered the question...the challenge." He prodded, his gaze roving over her body in anticipation.

"Not today." April focused on a bright yellow dandelion, and then picked it to get a closer look.

He laughed. "Afraid you'll lose control if you see me naked?"

"Afraid *you'll* lose control when you see *me*..." she laughed, running the dandelion along the back of his hand.

"You might be right. I still say you're a prude," he teased.

"Shy...s'all. Besides, I don't think I want to be naked with you."

"Makes one of us ..." he snickered, snatching the dandelion from her hand, then sticking it over her ear in her hair and patting it in place.

"So Mr. Hot and Cold is running hot about me now, eh?"

"Hotter than Hades in the sun," he said. His fingers grazed her cheek.

"Go ahead. Jump in. Who's stopping you?" April grabbed his hand, moved it away from her face and ran her thumb over his knuckles.

"Don't trust you not to run off with my clothes, Springtime. Come on, Venus, time to head home." Gavin got to his feet and extended his hand to April, helping her up.

Chewing the last mouthful of tasty grass, the horse pulled her head up and turned around under Gavin's direction. He led them to a downed tree trunk, where they mounted the horse. Venue returned them to the trail through the woods. April was grateful to leave the burning sunshine behind.

When they got back to the fence, Gavin dismounted first and helped April down.

"Where have you been?" She asked him.

"Around." Gavin avoided her questioning gaze.

"Not around me."

"Giving you some space until you settle with...whoever he is. Oh, yes, the dead guy."

"He's not dead."

"Why do I have the feeling I'm going to wish he was?" Gavin asked as he walked with Venus toward the barn.

BY NINE-THIRTY ON SATURDAY night, April had given up on Rusty. It was dark outside except for a full moon. She fed Romeo and padded barefoot into the bedroom, guided by the moonlight streaming through the skylight. As she rolled over and closed her eyes, a soft knock on the door broke the silence of the night, startling her. Wearing her flimsy short nightie, she cracked open the door. There was Rusty, big as life, filling the doorframe, then pushing his way in, sporting his easy grin.

"Sugar Bear," he said.

He grabbed her in an enormous hug and held her tight. Tears flooded her eyes as

anger and sadness mixed in her heart. She rested her head on his shoulder and let his affection soothe her. His mouth sought hers in a passionate kiss as his hand traveled to her breast. She stepped back, pushing his hand away, and shook her head.

"Don't cry, Honey, I'm safe now. Come make love with your Bear. I've missed your

sweet body, Sugar Bear," he said stepping closer to her.

April backed up.

"You come in here and...do you know what happened to me?"

He shook his head.

"Maybe you weren't injured in the explosion, but I was. I broke a couple of ribs, got a

concussion. I was in the hospital. Did you even care?"

"I'm so sorry, Honey, I didn't know. Honest."

"Why didn't you know? You didn't check up on me? You don't care, do you? How did

the explosion happen? Did you plan it? Why didn't you tell me? I have so many questions and all you want is to make love. Forget it," she said, crossing her arms, staring at him with angry eyes.

"Okay, okay. I'll explain."

She made a cup of tea and then sat down, dunking the bag in the hot water, waiting.

"I'm listening," she said, crossing her legs and arms.

"You know I've wanted to move to Mexico and open a bar, right?"

"And?"

"I don't have family like you do. My mom's an alcoholic and my dad's in jail. I have to

do it myself. An opportunity came up when I was in New York."

"What kind of opportunity?"

"I'm getting there," he said, opening the refrigerator and taking out a beer.

"I met these two guys, Juan and Caleb, in a bar in New York."

"I thought you dropped off your cargo, loaded up and came right back."

"Sometimes. Other times, I had a couple of hours to kill. So I met these guys and they

wanted to expand their...business into Allentown, but they needed transport."

"What kind of business?"

"Drugs. Nothing lethal like heroine, just pot, coke and stuff. So I agreed to truck their

stuff to their seller in Allentown."

"You were transporting *drugs?* Oh, Rusty! How could you?"

"I wasn't selling or anything. Just put a bag in the back of the truck and gave it to some

guy when I got home. They paid me a lot of money."

"Rusty..." she said, shading her eyes with her hand.

"It was a pretty good business. But sometimes I couldn't bring the money to them for a

couple of days, until I got another run to New York. They were cool. So I started to think, if they could wait four days for the money, well, I could take off with it and get a big head start. I saved up half what I needed. Then there was a big sale, sixty grand. Exactly what I needed to complete my plan."

"You didn't!"

"I did. I took the money and staged my death."

April gasped, her hand flew to her mouth as she stared at him wide-eyed. Rusty took a

swig of his beer as the silence enveloped them. April was motionless while Rusty's words penetrated her brain.

"You ripped off drug dealers?"

"Hey, it's drug money. Why shouldn't I have it instead? I would take me ten years to

save up enough for my dream. Now I have it."

"They'll kill you!"

"They think I'm dead," he said, smiling.

"What...what are you...?"

"Where's your diary, Sugar?"

April stared at him. "What's my diary got to do with anything?"

"Do you still have it?"

"Of course."

"Please get it, Sugar Bear."

She went into her room and returned with the book, handing it to him. He opened it and

paged to the back. There was a small key taped to the inside back cover. He let out a big sigh and pulled the key loose.

"What's that?" April asked.

"The key to the storage locker where the money is. Sweet! Now I can rock and roll."

She stood motionless. "You only came back here for the key...not for me," she said, tears

pricking her eyes.

"No, honey. Not true," he said, grabbing her quickly and hugging her.

"And I thought you truly loved me, worried about letting you down easy when all the

time it was only about...about this key...not me," she cried, tears coursing down her face.

"I do love you, April. I'd be here even without the key," Rusty said, folding her in his

arms.

She struggled to get away from him but he held her fast, kissing her hair. "April, honey, I

came for both. Don't you want to go to Mexico with me?"

"As a fugitive? A thief? A drug runner?"

"Come on, April. It's not so bad. They deserved it. Now I'm going straight. We can

work the bar together. You always said you wanted to go to faraway places...Mexico?"

"Not in a million years, Rusty."

She went into the bedroom and slipped into her bathrobe. As she was leaving the

room, she picked her engagement ring off the dresser. When April returned to the living room, she took Rusty's hand, opened it flat and placed the ring on it, then closed his fingers around it.

"Take it. You can sell it."

"You're...breaking our engagement?"

She nodded.

"I knew you wouldn't come with me," he admitted, closing his hand on the ring.

"How did you know? I had agreed to marry you."

"I know...because of our life in Allentown. You say you want an adventurous life,

April, but you're kidding yourself."

"How can you say that?"

"Because of Allentown. We had a great life there...you made it great. You made a

home for us, fixed up our little apartment so nice, cooked great meals, made love whenever I wanted, I couldn't wait to get home to you from New York. You're a nester, April. So I wanted to marry you, thinking the bar would take a long time to happen and we could be happy the way we were. But things changed..."

"I did nest, didn't I?" A smile crept over her face as she looked at him.

"Yeah, and it was super. Sure would like to get some of your great lovin' again, Sugar

Bear...you look mighty fine in..." he said, coming closer to her.

She held her hand up to ward him off and backed away. "Stay away," she warned.

"You know I'd never force you to sleep with me, honey. Don't be afraid. If you

don't want to, it's okay."

"Thanks," she said, dropping her gaze to the floor.

"I love you, April, but I don't think you'd be happy in Mexico."

"On the run? I couldn't live with the...history, Rusty."

"Don't you want to keep the ring?" He opened his hand and held it out to her.

"You take it. Some day you might need to sell it," she said, curling his big fingers around

the small jewel.

Rusty leaned down and kissed her, running his hand down her hair.

"You sure about the...lovin'?"

"I am."

"You have someone else? Are you sleepin' with someone else?"

"Why do you ask?"

"You never turned me down before."

"Maybe you're not the man I thought you were. The man I was in love with wouldn't

have deserted me when I was hurt...or broken the law."

"I am sorry, April. I kept you out of it so you'd be safe. If you didn't know about this, then you couldn't get hurt...but I guess it backfired and you got hurt anyway."

"Right."

"I know it's hard for you to understand but I don't have any backup. I have to take care

of myself, April. Sometimes people do things...they might not otherwise do...you know, I'm not going to run drugs again. The opportunity was there...I couldn't help it. I hope you understand."

She looked at his sad expression and the ring which appeared so tiny in his large hand

and regretted her actions.

"We had an adventure together, didn't we?" he asked her.

April crossed the room and embraced him. He held her tight, planting small kisses on

her hair while she sighed.

"We were good together," April admitted.

They broke and Rusty finished his beer. "So who is this guy?" he asked, looking at her keenly. April blushed.

"I know there's someone, April, so stop pretending. You talk about grieving, but it didn't take you long after you thought I was dead to find someone else, did it?"

Her blush deepened because what he said was true. "It doesn't matter now," she said, avoiding his gaze.

"I should have expected a beautiful woman like you wouldn't be alone long."

"I did grieve for you...but then you told me you were alive..."

"Hey, it's okay. I deserve it. I'm lucky you weren't waiting for me with a shotgun. I hope he loves you as much as I have and he treats you good."

"I did love you, Rusty...I'm sorry it's turned out this way," she said, slipping her arms around him one more time.

April looked up at him and saw a wave of sadness pass over his face before he recovered his usual jovial way.

"Me, too," he said, holding her.

"I have appointments tomorrow, it's past my bedtime," April said, backing away.

"Appointments on Sunday?"

"I'm organizing a charity art auction on Labor Day and I'm meeting with a church group tomorrow.

"Organizing...always organizing." He chuckled. "I learned a lot from you about organizing, Sugar Bear. I never would've been able to pull this off before I met you. Now, I'll be off to my new life before anyone catches on. And I have you to thank."

"I don't know if what you're saying is good or bad."

"It's good, honey. It's all good. So which side of the bed is yours?" he asked.

"You're in this room," she said, showing him to Cassie's old room.

He made a face. "Sugar Bear...please?"

"Rusty, I don't love you anymore. I didn't want to tell you but you keep pushing. Please stop. It's not going to happen."

"Are you sleeping with him?"

April looked away from him, shook her head and gazed out the window but couldn't stop a blush from creeping up her neck.

Rusty snickered. "Huh. Poor guy. Doesn't know what he's missing."

The blush increased, turning her face a hot pink.

"Do you love him?" He asked, sinking down on the sofa placing his empty beer bottle on the coffee table.

"I don't know...maybe," April said, picking up his bottle and putting it in the sink.

"Does he love you?" Rusty ran his fingers through his hair and followed her.

"Don't know." She rinsed out the bottle and turned to look at him.

"He'd be stupid not to. He lives here?"

She nodded.

"This might be the perfect place for you, April."

"Maybe…maybe not."

"If I can't have you…I hope this guy appreciates what he's got. If he doesn't, let me know and I'll come around and *remind* him for you," Rusty said, clenching his hand into a fist and pounding it into his palm.

April smiled, remembering how he saved her on the road when her tire blew, how he was always protective. Relieved to know she hadn't totally misjudged how he regarded her, April touched his arm and looked into his eyes. He still cared about her.

They went to their own rooms and turned out the lights. April tossed and turned, restless with much on her mind. At five o'clock in the morning, Rusty arose, packed his backpack, made a pot of coffee and was ready to leave by five thirty. April got out of bed, put on her robe and padded into the kitchen to join him before he left.

They walked out onto the deck, stepping softly so as not to disturb the quiet of the early morning. April saddened to see him leave. Although she knew she could never be happy going to Mexico with him, she'd miss him.

"I'm taking my cell phone. You can always reach me there, if you need me," he said.

"Okay," she said. Then it was time for him to leave. Rusty took her in his arms for a long hug and a very passionate kiss. April softened against him, wondering if this would be the last time she would ever see him. They broke, he patted her behind affectionately and slipped quietly up the embankment and into his car. April waved. On her way back to the cabin, she sighed. Free, for the first time in months.

Chapter Ten

At five o'clock in the morning, while April and Rusty were sipping coffee, Gavin climbed up on top of the firehouse to look for eagles. He knew Rusty was due to visit April and he couldn't sleep thinking about what was going on between them.

At five thirty, he spanned the area with the binocs and caught Rusty and April in an embrace on the deck. His heart stopped beating as he watched the two former lovers bid each other a fond farewell. Jealousy tightened in his chest. Anger choked his throat.

So, Rusty and April had spent the night together. She had resisted Gavin but the minute this guy had showed up, she'd jumped into the sack with him. Gavin could feel red fury climb his neck. He watched until Rusty drove away and April went back inside.

At six o'clock, Gavin went to The Luncheonette to have breakfast before he confronted her. He wasn't used to playing second fiddle and he didn't plan to start now. He'd thought of her as his, not to be shared but to be cherished by him alone. Apparently she didn't understand. Perhaps now was the time to make this clear.

JUAN AND CALEB WERE in the car by six am to make an early start back to New York City. They stopped at Al's gas station in Allentown, the one located on the road leading to the highway. Caleb got out to pump gas, while Juan went inside to buy some supplies.

"Say Al, you remember the big guy, Rusty?"

Al nodded as he totaled up water, chips and beer on the cash register.

"Sure and his girlfriend. What a piece she was...boy!"

"Yeah, yeah, I know. What was her name? Remember?"

Al stopped his fingers on the register before totaling it up. He put his hand flat down on the counter and looked up at the ceiling, his brow furrowed.

"Let me see...Rusty and...and...April! That's it! April something."

"Don't remember her last name, do you?"

"Naw...don't think—wait. It was something Irish, no, Scottish...a Mc-something, I think."

"Know what happened to her?"

"She was hurt when Rusty's car blew up but I have no idea what happened to her. I think they lived on Forsythe Street or DeKalb...somewhere."

"Thanks, Al," Juan said, tossing a credit card at the man after he totaled up the purchases.

"No problem. Have a good trip. Should I tell April you're looking for her, if I see her?"

"Not necessary. We only wanted to pay our condolences."

"Nice of you boys. Friends of Rusty's?

"Co-workers, you might say."

"It's too bad about what happened to him. Now she's alone."

"Exactly the way we feel, Al. We'd like to tell her how sorry we are."

"Nice, buddy, real nice. I'm sure she'd appreciate it."

"Thanks for the info," Juan said, scooping up the black plastic bag and heading toward the door.

Caleb waited in the car with the engine running. Juan got in the front next to him and turned to face him.

"April. April Mc-something."

"It's a start," Caleb said.

"You bet it is," Juan said, putting the car in gear and turning out on-to the street.

AT SEVEN O'CLOCK, GAVIN showed up outside April's cabin, where he found Romeo on the deck, howling for his breakfast. Gavin petted the cat then went inside to get cat food letting the door slam, too angry to be concerned about waking up April.

She peeked out of her room, rubbing her eyes. "Gavin? You scared me," she said, coming out to get the makings for Romeo's meal down from the cabinet.

"Sorry. Didn't mean to wake you...seeing as you had such a busy...active night."

"What do you mean?"

His gaze roamed slowly over her form, barely covered by the night-ie. Suddenly she felt naked and retreated to the bedroom, returning wearing her robe.

"I saw him. Saw him leave," Gavin replied when she joined him in the kitchen.

"Who? Rusty?"

"I guess. Unless you are sleeping with a lot of other men I don't know about."

"Whoa! I'm not sleeping with anyone," April said, grabbing Romeo's full food dish and pushing through the screen door.

"I saw him leave here at five-thirty this morning. He spent the night here."

"So?" She straightened up and faced him.

"So, I assume you slept with him."

"Don't assume."

"Didn't you?"

She shook her head.

Angry, jealous and frustrated, Gavin strode through the door and into the smaller bedroom where Rusty spent the night. April was right on his heels.

"Doesn't look like anyone slept here," he said, pointing to the perfectly made up bed, then leaving the room and entering April's bedroom.

"Looks like a lot of action went on here, though," Gavin said, gesturing to her torn apart bed. A victorious gleam appeared in his eye, a rueful smile on his lips.

"I was restless," she explained, biting a cuticle.

"I'll bet you were. I've heard it called lots of things, April, but 'restless' is a new one," he said, turning a cold stare on her. Jealousy rose in his chest.

"You've got to believe me. Rusty made his bed...maybe for the first time in his life, but he did. He didn't sleep in this bed with me. We didn't make love. Honestly."

"You want me to believe a guy you lived with consented to stay here with you without sex?" He moved toward the door.

"Exactly," she said, putting her hand on his arm

Gavin made a disgusted noise and walked outside. "I'm only a fireman, April, but I'm not stupid."

"You don't trust me? Don't believe me?"

"I don't trust him. I know men." He ran his hand through his hair.

She felt helpless as tears stung at the back of her eyes but she refused to give in.

"I'm telling you, I didn't sleep with him and my word should be good enough for you." April clutched his arms in a tight grip, forcing him to face her angry eyes.

"Your *word?* You lied to me about him from the beginning. Why should I believe you now?" Gavin flipped her hands off his arms in one gesture and backed up. April moved toward him quickly.

"Because I'm telling the truth. Don't you know me well enough yet to know when I'm telling the truth?" She implored moving toward him, tears threatening to spill onto her cheeks. She reached out to touch him.

"When I heard about this guy, I realized I didn't know you well at all...even though I thought I did," he said, jumping back as if her hand were a red-hot poker.

"Please," she said, putting her face in her hands to muffle a sob and hide her tears.

"I'd like to," he said, softening for a moment, putting his hand on her shoulder," but the way you kissed him before he left says otherwise."

"Please Gavin, you have to believe me," she said, taking his arm.

He pulled away from her. "I have work to do," he said, moving toward the stairs.

"He's gone," she revealed, desperate to get him back.

"Gone where?" He halted at the top step, reconsidering.

"To Mexico." April moved slowly closer to him.

"Are going to go with him?" Gavin asked, remaining paused.

"He left already," she replied, looking at a small puddle on the deck.

"Are you going to join him there?" He asked.

"No."

"I don't believe you. You hate this town, this life. Mexico is the perfect, exotic place for you. I hope you'll both be very happy there," he said, descending the stairs quickly, anxious to get away.

Gavin jammed the truck into gear and pulled away, seeing her image grow smaller in the rearview mirror as he drove on, half wanting her to follow him and half wanting to be alone to think. He was in love and in pain, a bad combination.

APRIL WENT TO HER MEETINGS on Sunday but couldn't concentrate. Rusty was gone and now Gavin, too. She didn't know what to do. April dissolved into tears several times during the day. She was exhausted, in love, sad, confused, and lonely.

Monday morning, she awoke at seven. While toting garbage to the Dumpster, she spotted something black. As she got closer the black something reared up, looked at her and roared. April froze as the mother black bear and her two cubs continued going through the garbage. Trembling, the young women averted her gaze. The mother bear stood still, watching her. Slowly, April backed away, taking tiny steps. After moving twenty feet back, the mother bear apparently no longer saw her as a threat, and she took her cubs and lumbered back into the woods.

April ran back to her cabin, her feet fairly flying over the turf, and shut the door. Hal came over. When she saw him, she launched herself into his arms crying hysterically.

"You're okay, April," Hal said, patting her back. "Shirley and I watched you through the window."

She wiped her face with a paper towel. "I'm still shaking."

"You did the right thing," Hal said, pouring her a cup of coffee and then one for himself.

"I was so scared," she admitted.

"We saw that. But you're all right now. Do you have a gun? Nothing too high-powered, enough to scare a bear away with?"

She shook her head. "I'm afraid of guns."

"I'll bet Gavin does. He could lend you one, and maybe teach you to shoot."

"He's not speaking to me right now."

"Have a fight?"

"It's complicated. I've got people to see about the auction..."

"Go around and see Gavin. I'm sure he'll help you."

She was too scared to be alone so Shirley and Hal took her into their cabin for the day. April made phone calls while the couple went about their usual routine, Shirley made lunch and her husband read.

Hal offered to take the two women out to dinner. They went to Homer's for burgers by the lake. April was grateful for their friendship. During dinner, they urged her to turn to Gavin for help.

"He knows how to shoot. I'm sure he'd help you," Shirley said, taking a forkful of lettuce.

"He's crazy for you, April. He'd never let anything happen to you," Hal put in.

After dinner, April got up the courage to talk to Gavin. She went by his house but he wasn't there. She guessed he might be on the roof of the firehouse, a place he liked to go to think. Thunder sounded in the distance. A storm was rolling in. It was a hot day and April welcomed the relief a shower would provide, cooling things off.

As she'd expected, Gavin stood on the fire station roof, looking up at the sky. She climbed the fire escape to the second floor then continued another flight to the roof. The thunder grew louder and a vein of light streaked down from the sky. She shivered, nervous to get so high up during an electrical storm. But she was there, so she might as well go through with it. She called to him and he turned around.

"What are you doing here?" he asked, putting down the binoculars.

"I've come to ask a favor."

"You got a lot of nerve."

"I need your help." She put her hands behind her back and shifted her weight.

"What for?"

"There was a bear, a black bear at the Dumpster this morning when I went with the garbage and she had two cubs with her..."

"A mother bear can be dangerous. You shouldn't be anywhere near a mother with her cubs," he warned.

"I know. She was raiding the trash. Hal suggested I get a gun and learn how to shoot. But I'm afraid of guns..." she said, biting her cuticle.

"Why don't you call on your boyfriend to help you?"

"Come on, Gavin. Not fair."

"I've got a .22 semi-automatic. I suppose I could lend it to you. Do you know how to use a gun?" He moved closer to her.

She shook her head. A loud clap of thunder startled her. April screamed and jumped into Gavin's arms. Lightning flashed a few seconds later, lighting up the sky, and April hid her face in his shoulder. Then the heavens opened up. Rain poured down, so thick it was like a wall of water cascaded down upon them. April and Gavin were quickly soaked through, as if someone had dumped a bucket of water over their heads.

Water ran in rivulets down her face and matted her hair to her head. Gavin's blue T-shirt stuck to his chest. Water soaked his eyelashes, causing them to clump together, giving his eyes a black look. April folded one arm across her chest, trying to keep her T-shirt dry; however it was soaked through almost immediately. After only moments in the rain, their shorts were almost as wet as their shirts.

Gavin's jean shorts hung low and heavy on his hips, while April's lightweight dark pink cotton shorts clung to her curves. She knew her clothing showed way too much. She tugged at the fabric, freeing first from one leg, then the other. Fortunately, the color kept them from being see-through. The temperature dropped several degrees in a matter of minutes. She shivered, clinging to Gavin for warmth, though he was obviously uncomfortable with her in his arms.

She stepped back, aware he didn't want her so close. His hungry gaze landed on her breasts. April glanced down to see her white T-shirt and bra had become nearly transparent. Embarrassed, she folded her arms across her chest again. His shirt seemed to disappear in the rain, outlining the strong muscles of his chest. April couldn't help herself as she stared at him in frank admiration.

"Our own private wet T-shirt contest," she joked.

He smiled. "You win," he said, staring at her chest.

Her face flushed and she turned away from him. He took her by the shoulder and turned her around, pulling her into his arms for a passionate kiss. Thunder continued to rumble. Rain fell on them at a record rate, but the lightning stopped. The wetter they got, the more passionate their embrace as Gavin's reserve dissolved in the downpour. He took April's face in his hands as he probed her mouth with his tongue. She stepped closer to him and wound her arms around his neck, losing her hands in his wet hair as excitement built. His arms lowered to her waist and held her close, his fingers fanned out on her bottom. Their shirts were completely joined by wetness, as if it were raining glue. A sheet of paper wouldn't fit between them. As his tongue teased hers, she felt herself melting into his kiss, her body yielding. He covered her breast with his fingers. When she didn't pull away, he squeezed gently, filling his hand with her softness. A moan escaped from her mouth...desire shot through her at his touch.

Before their hunger for each other took over, Gavin came to his senses and backed away. A rush of cold air chilled them. April stood still, her pulse racing, as she watched his heavy breathing. She covered her chest with her arms. He raised his hand to her face and traced two raindrops down her cheek with his forefinger before speaking.

"I'm sorry, I shouldn't have...I forgot you belong to somebody else," he said.

April's tears mixed with wetness falling from the sky, making them invisible to Gavin. She raised the back of her hand to her lips and turned to go but he grabbed her arm, stopping her.

"I'll give you the rifle...and shooting lessons, too. Can't have you mauled by a bear and people saying it's my fault."

She nodded her thanks, unable to speak before walking to the ladder. April turned for one last look and saw him as he watched her leave, desire in his eyes and regret on his face. She wished she could find words to convince him of her feelings but as she hesitated, his face harden into a mask, impenetrable and wary. Sadness filled her heart.

WHEN GAVIN GOT TO THE yellow house, he went in the back door, which was never locked. In the mud room, he undressed, slung a towel over his shoulder, and wrapped another around his waist. Then he dropped his soaking clothes in the washer in the next room.

His aunt was placing a pie in the oven when he entered the kitchen "Were you out in the storm? On the roof again? With lightning? That's dangerous."

Gavin ignored her.

'Your aunt is right, Gavin. When there's lightning, you gotta take cover, son."

"I know, I know,"

"Did the young lady find you? She came here lookin' for ya," Laura said, moving into the living room to open the windows she had closed during the storm

Gavin nodded silently.

"You were out in the rain with her? She get soaked, too? Wet T-shirt contest?" Barney asked, his eyes glistening.

Laura smacked Barney gently in the arm with a newspaper she was carrying.

"Mind out of the gutter, Barney," she said, moving into the other room.

Barney laughed but Gavin didn't join him.

"Don't talk about April like that, Uncle Barney," Gavin said, irritated.

"Oh? This one's different, huh?" Barney teased.

Gavin rubbed his torso and hair with the spare towel but didn't respond.

"She the one, Gavin?" Barney asked.

Gavin continued to dry off and ignored Barney.

"How about a hot tea or hot chocolate, son?" Laura asked him.

"Hot chocolate sounds good, Aunt Laura," he said, moving toward the stairs, "I'll be right back."

The sound of lowered voices stopped Gavin halfway up the stairs to his apartment. He halted long enough to listen to the exchange between his aunt and uncle.

"Barney, don't tease him. I think he's in love. She may be the one. Let him be."

"You're too sensitive, Laura. He's a guy. Guys joke about women."

"Not about their wives."

"Never, no, never about your wife."

"So listen to what he's *not* tellin' you. He isn't jokin' about this one."

"You may be right, Laura. He sure isn't jokin' about her."

"So you don't joke either. Wouldn't want him to take a poke at you. At your age, who knows what'd get broken," she said laughing.

"The one? I wish," he muttered as he crept silently up the last few steps.

APRIL GOT HOME AS HER landline was ringing.

Sunny's voice greeted her. "Checking to make sure you're okay."

"I got soaked."

"You were out in this?"

April sighed and kicked off her wet shoes. "I went to see Gavin...on the roof of the firehouse," she said, peeling off her wet shorts with one hand while she held the phone with the other.

"You shouldn't be up there when there is lightning."

"I know."

"Do you have enough candles and flashlights? Storms sometimes cause power outages, like a tree knocking out the power lines."

"I'll check. Thanks for the heads up."

"What's happening with you and Gavin anyway?"

"I don't know. Rusty came to see me. Gavin saw him leave and...well...things are a mess."

"I'm sorry," Sunny said.

A heavy silence settled over their conversation as April struggled to control her emotions. After taking several deep breaths, she continued.

"At least I have the auction." said April

"Come over tomorrow and give me an update," Sunny said, "I'm heading to bed."

"Goodnight."

April hung up the phone. She felt alone as the thunder continued to rage outside and rain pelted the skylights and the roof. She changed into dry clothes then heard a meow. Romeo was at the door. When she opened it, the wet cat scampered inside. April fed him and dried him with a towel. She curled up in bed with a book. Romeo was a comfort, cuddled up at her side, asleep, and purring loudly.

At least there's one male left who wants to be with me.

Chapter Eleven

Breakfast was early on the day of the town garage sale. Laura spent three days organizing things she wanted to sell, even swiping some old tools from Barney's tool shed to go with the linens, china, books, clothing and CD's she'd put aside. Gavin had pledged the day to her, offering to help her set up, using his truck to deliver large treasures to people, lift, cart, haul and man the table while Laura took a few short breaks.

"Everything is in the living room, Gavin, except for a few things on the front lawn," Laura said.

"Your girlfriend coming to the sale today?" Barney asked, taking a bite of his French toast.

"She's not my girlfriend," Gavin said, pointedly, before taking a gulp of his coffee.

"Excuse me, son, but you've been spending a lot of time with her...seems to me..."

"She belongs to someone else."

Laura and Barney looked at each other then down at their plates as they continued to eat. Silence filled the room.

"She isn't married, is she?" Laura asked, breaking a piece of toast in half.

Gavin shook his head.

"Then, heck, son, she's fair game! If he hasn't put a ring on her finger, she's available," Barney said.

"Not like you to let a little competition get in your way," Laura said.

"It's her choice."

"For a smart girl, she's pretty dumb," Laura sniffed.

Gavin finished his food and put his dish in the sink. "I'm going start moving the stuff downtown," he said. "Great breakfast, Aunt Laura."

She nodded to him before he moved through the doorway to the living room.

On his way, Gavin stopped to rummage through a drawer in the front hall, looking for a cap. It was forecast to be a hot day and he needed protection from the sun. While his hand felt for the headgear, his ears picked up the conversation drifting out from the kitchen.

"Breaks my heart."

"Don't give up on him, Laura. I ain't met the filly yet, can resist our boy," Barney replied.

"Maybe you're right," Laura said.

"Hope so, Barney," Gavin murmured to himself as he walked out the front door.

It was a beautiful, sunny day and little downtown Pine Grove was filling up with folding tables and secondhand wares. Laura Dailey had sworn to her nephew she'd have a prettier table than Alma Phillips this year—not an easy task. She brought her best cloths to cover the cheap tables but she was not artistic and didn't have a knack for arranging things to look their best. Alma watched with smug confidence as Laura moved things around, uncertain where they should go. Gavin lounged in the shade slurping an iced coffee and looking around.

Movement in the distance caught his eye and the sun glinting off April's shiny dark hair had him straightening in his seat.

April, Sunny, and Karen sauntered down the street, whispering secrets, giggling and pointing at various displays until April spied Gavin. She stopped laughing and gave him a cool nod. He returned it. Sunny smiled at him and waved as she led her companions over to Laura Dailey's.

"Sunny, I don't know what to do," said Laura. "Alma's table looks so pretty. Every year she has the best-looking table. I have better merchandise, but I can't seem to make it look as nice."

"I think I can help," April offered, stepping over to the tables.

Gavin stood up and inched his way over to watch April. She took a second tablecloth and smoothed it artfully over the first angling it so the colors and patterns from both cloths were visible.

She stacked linens attractively, layering them and fanning them out so a bit of each design peeped out, grouped serving pieces, bunched dried flowers, put them in pitchers and vases and spread items over the tables so they didn't look crowded. When she was done the display outclassed Alma Phillips' table by a mile.

"Why, look at that! April, you're a genius! My table looks better than Alma's," Laura said, her eyes glowing with pride.

April smiled at Laura and glanced at Gavin.

"Come back for some of my apple pie in a bit...and some iced tea, too." Laura offered, patting her hand.

"I will, thank you."

April sauntered over to Gavin.

"Will you be here when I get back?"

"Not if I can help it," he shot back.

She stepped back as if slapped.

Laura gasped. "Gavin!"

"I might be delivering something or doing something else, Aunt Laura," Gavin said, trying to make his curt response appear reasonable. He wanted desperately to see April again but wouldn't admit it, not to her or even to himself. Trying to keep his distance wasn't working as she crept into his mind and took over his heart.

"Still. That's no way to speak to April. She only asked you a question."

"She never just asks me a question...do you, April?"

With a blush the young woman turned away.

"See? She's checking up on me..."

Laura's attention was diverted by a customer.

"After the way you kissed and...touched me in the rain, Gavin Dailey, I'd think you'd be nicer," she whispered, putting her face right up into his.

"A mistake. I told you." But he didn't move away from her.

"Didn't seem like a mistake to me. Seemed like you knew exactly what you were doing, trying to seduce me." April put her hands on her hips but remained in his face.

"I wasn't...I lost my head for a moment. You were practically naked. Don't make it into something it wasn't. Besides, you weren't exactly resisting me," he said, with a wicked grin.

April blushed and turned away from him. "Such a nasty thing to say," she retorted when she found her voice.

"Why? Because you wanted it...wanted me? The truth..." he whispered.

April gave a tiny shake when a chill went up her spine as his warm breath caressed her ear. "That's what you think?"

"That's what I *know*." He stared at her, challenging her to deny it.

"You wanted me first," she retorted.

"I've wanted you since I saw you wearing nothing but a towel. But you *belong* to someone else."

"I don't *belong* to anybody," she muttered.

Desire flowed through him as he stared at her.

"April! Meet me down at Celia's table," Sunny called.

KAREN DRAGGED SUNNY away to see Celia Carson's table, loaded with baby clothes and toys. April stopped next to Justin at the bake sale table in front of the ambulance corps. She bought a brownie and ate it quickly before it melted in the sun, chatting with Justin while she chewed. From time to time, she glanced at Gavin, as Justin pumped her for information on Cassie's return.

"I don't know when she's coming back. I'm sorry," she murmured. "I've only received one post card from Paris.

Justin groaned. "Paris! She's in Paris? French guys'll be crawling all over her."

"She's pretty stuck on you, Justin. I wouldn't worry." April smiled and patted him on the shoulder.

"Easy for you to say. Your squeeze is right here in town."

"Mine?"

"Gavin. Is there someone else?"

April blushed. Out of the corner of her eye, she could see Gavin watching them with interest. When Justin started selling baked goods and iced coffee to other customers, April wandered away. The sun grew hotter at midday, she strolled down the street, stopping at different tables, pretending to be interested in what they were selling but feeling uncomfortable as sweat trickled down her back, between her breasts, and beaded on her forehead.

All she could think about was Gavin. She glanced his way from time to time, catching his eye occasionally. She was conflicted. She wanted him but with him came this small town, her dreams of exotic places would vanish along with her desire for adventure. She laughed ruefully at her over-confidence, assuming she had a future with Gavin. He didn't trust her right now, whatever they had had together was in serious jeopardy if not gone already.

Was Rusty right? Was she a nester, fooling herself into thinking she'd be happy moving from strange country to strange country?

She caught up with Karen and Sunny, who were chattering away about children and inspecting everything. Not wishing to ruin Sunny's day, and trying to escape the heat, April searched for a shady spot to get relief. If Sunny noticed, she didn't say anything.

At lunch time, the women found a table in the shade in front of Homer's restaurant, where they munched on burgers and drank lemonade. Not having much appetite, April gave half of hers to Sunny, who was ravenous.

Lonely, distracted and uncomfortably warm April wandered over to the lake and looked out at the people swimming and fishing. She felt a sudden urge to run off the end of the Webster's dock and jump in the cool water, clothes and all, but she resisted, not wishing to make a spectacle of herself. On her way back to join Karen and Sunny, she stopped and looked at some clothes at the Webster's' table. She eyed a short, pink terry cloth robe.

"April, you want this?" Essie Webster asked.

"How much?"

"Free...for you. You're doing so much for us with the art auction. Take it, dear."

The plump, gray-haired woman put it in a bag and pushed it into April's arms.

"Thank you, Essie."

She wiped her forehead with the back of her hand, took the bag and stopped. She glanced at Sunny and Karen, then at Gavin, watching her from his chair perched in the shade, a plate of half-eaten Laura Dailey fried chicken and homemade cole slaw on his lap. The sun beat down on April, making her sweat as much as Gavin's stare.

She gave him a defiant smile, cocked an eyebrow, and turned. She ran down to the dock and stopped, looking back to check if Gavin had followed her. Yep, there he was. She dropped the bag with the robe in it on the edge, slipped off her shoes and backed up. Gavin drew closer, his eyebrows knitted.

She flashed him an impish grin and took off, running full speed. At the end of the dock, she dove into the water, sundress and all. She came up, paddled to the dock, wiggled out of the dress, which she shoved up on the dry wood, next to the bag, and swam half-naked in the lake. The water swirled around her legs and breasts, cooling her as she went under, then came up again, pushing her hair out of her eyes, swimming then treading water. She felt free, cool...wonderful.

By now, Gavin stood on the edge. She returned to the dock and looked up at him.

"What're you doing?" he asked.

"What does it look like? Swimming. Its hot today."

"You're not...you don't have a bathing suit."

"So what?"

"There are tons of people here and they're looking at you."

"They can't see anything. They should mind their own business. I wanted to cool off. Who's the prude now?"

Gavin stood there, watching. The water was inviting. Sweat clung to the back of his neck. April laughed, splashing around. He pulled his shirt off.

"Oh no you don't! Gavin Dailey, don't you dare come in here with me," April warned.

A wicked grin spread across his face as he unzipped his shorts.

"Gavin!" April shouted.

He dropped them and jumped in wearing only his boxers, splashing April in the face. With a gasp, she headed toward the dock and pulled herself up the ladder. Halfway up, she reached over for the bag, plucked the robe out and donned it quickly, before Gavin could reach her.

"You're right. The water feels great!" He said, grinning.

Their impromptu swim seemed to dissolve the tension between them. He swam to the float and back, then pulled himself up the ladder. He slipped his shorts back on and sat shirtless in the sun. April plopped down, cross-legged, next to him, wrapped in her new robe. She spread out her wet dress to dry.

"I guess you're not the only spontaneous person in Pine Grove," he said.

"I guess not," she laughed.

She stared at him, watching water drip down his hard chest, and off his dark hair onto his face. He had never looked more appealing, April averted her eyes from his lips. She wanted to wipe the water off his face and chest with her hand but didn't dare. Instead she drew her knees up to her chest, wrapping her arms around them.

"The sun'll dry my dress quickly."

"You can dress in Homer's."

She nodded, unable to look away from him.

Sunny and Karen caught up.

"Quite a feat, miss," said Karen.

"I needed to cool off," April said, a grin spreading across her face.

Karen looked at Gavin and back at April. "I can see why."

April blushed and looked away.

Sunny and Karen chuckled when Gavin gave them a quizzical look. The two ladies wandered off to finish perusing the tables, leaving Gavin and April alone.

"I've got to get back. Aunt Laura needs a break," he said rising and extending his hand to her. She pulled hard on his arm to stand up. When she jumped up, he fell backward and took them into the lake again. The soaking wet terry robe became very heavy, weighing April down before she could slip out of it. She fell under the water, struggling to rise to the surface. April managed to wriggle out of the robe, and bobbed up, dragging the soggy garment behind her. Gavin's his face lit up when he saw her. "There you are. You okay?" He asked, swimming to her.

She nodded and started laughing. She tried to wring out the robe, not managing to get much water out of the dense fabric. She wrapped it around herself anyway, and Gavin helped her up the ladder his shorts sagging a bit, weighed down by wetness. They sat on the dock and laughed until they cried. April snatched up her dress and went into Homer's to change.

Gavin returned to his aunt's table.

"What happened to you?" she asked.

"Swimming or falling in, take your pick," he replied.

Gavin took over the table, giving Laura a break. April joined Sunny and Karen to finish their shopping. At four o'clock, Laura sent Gavin to bring April over for her pie and iced tea. The garage sale was winding down; people were packing up. Laura was half packed and stopped to share pie. Laura handed April a big slice.

"I sold more because of the way you arranged the tables, April. They looked beautiful. Thank you. Now I don't have to cart junk back into my house!" she laughed.

"You're welcome. This is the best apple pie I've ever eaten," the young woman said, lifting another forkful into her mouth.

Laura beamed. She was an outstanding cook and proud of it. Barney came by to help Gavin and Laura clean up. Mike came up behind Sunny and wrapped his arms around her middle pulling her into a hug. She leaned back into his shoulder and closed her eyes. The heat had worn her out and he'd come to drive her home.

"Laura, I'm taking you out to dinner tonight," Barney said.

"We can use the money I made today," she said, proudly holding up a wad of bills. Gavin watched Sunny and Mike, his aunt and uncle and wished he could be preparing to celebrate the end of a fun day with April, the woman he loved, too...but April wasn't his woman, not yet and maybe never would be.

"April, Gavin, Karen's family is having a big barbecue tomorrow night, do you want to come?" Sunny asked.

Trying not to look at each other but unable to avoid eye contact, they said "yes" at the same time.

April climbed into the back seat of Mike's car. and almost fell asleep on the ride home. When they dropped her off, Romeo was stretched out, dozing in a small shady spot on the deck. He meowed a greeting to April, rubbing up against her legs. She fed him, then fell asleep on her couch.

Monday evening, Gavin walked down the embankment to the cabin carrying
.22 SEMI-AUTOMATIC RIFLE.

"April!" he called out. As he got close, Romeo showed up on the deck railing and meowed loudly for food. April appeared in the doorway, cradling her cell on her ear while she opened the door.

"We have thirty artists participating so far. Yes, it is worthy of a piece in your paper. Why? What? Of course not. This is a legitimate charity function. Okay, I'll comp you a ticket...for *two* write-ups in your paper. Correct, *two!* No, no. Okay. Thank you. See you in a few weeks."

She hung up the phone, gave Gavin a quizzical look while she petted Romeo.

"Is it a coincidence...you both showing up at the same time?"

"Very funny. Here's the rifle. Time for a shooting lesson...unless you have a hot date or something?"

"*Ha Ha*! Romeo's been out tomcatting...what about you?" She asked him flirtatiously.

"In fifteen seconds I'm leaving...deal with the bear on your own."

"Okay, okay."

"You got an empty tin can? Something bigger than a can of cat food. I don't think you're ready to hit the bull's-eye your first time out."

"I might be Annie Oakley, for all you know, Gavin Dailey."

"Or you might be Mr. Magoo," he corrected with a snicker.

April disappeared inside and returned with an empty tin can. Gavin motioned for her to follow him as he wound through the woods until he found a clearing and a tree stump.

"Safety first. Here, this is the trigger, if you *don't* put your finger on the trigger, you *can't* fire the gun. See? Don't carry it like this." He held his finger over the trigger. Then he moved it off. "Hold it like this instead. Rest your finger alongside the trigger, not on it. Okay, now you hold it," he said, handing her the gun butt end first.

April held it gingerly, as if it would bite her. She looked it over, her brows knitted.

"It nothing to be afraid of. Point it down at the ground...not at your foot, April, at the ground. Walk around with it. Get comfortable."

She stomped around the clearing a little holding the gun stiffly at her side.

"Rest your finger *next* to the trigger, not on it, remember?"

She nodded and continued to walk around. Gavin motioned her over, took the gun and put it on the ground.

"This is a magazine. It holds the bullets. 'Cause this is an automatic, it fires five bullets in rapid succession...if you keep pulling the trigger, the gun will keep shooting. You won't need to reload or pull the bolt back or anything with this gun...not until the magazine is empty. I'm going to show you how to load it.'

They spent the next fifteen minutes putting bullets in the magazine. Gavin was a patient teacher, standing opposite April, not touching her. She followed his instructions without comment, concentrating on his words and avoiding his eyes.

Then he showed her how to insert the magazine into the gun. First they practiced with an empty one, then with a full one.

"Remember to rest your finger next to the trigger, not on it," he reminded her when she misplaced her finger again.

After she loaded the magazine correctly, April began to show a little confidence.

"This is the bolt. I pulled it back before I loaded the magazine and now you will release the bolt. It loads the bullet into the gun," Gavin explained.

By the time they were finished loading and releasing the bolt, it was almost too dark to shoot. Gavin was doing well, treating April like any other student, teaching her thoroughly without physical contact. But then it came time to shoulder the rifle and line up the sites.

"Hold the gun like this," he said, demonstrating the stance, nestling the rifle in his shoulder before handing the gun to her.

"Like this?" She asked, holding the rifle too low.

He shook his head and showed her again. This time she held it too high.

Again he took the rifle and demonstrated.

"Just show me, Gavin, please, before it's too dark to see," April pleaded.

Against his better judgment, Gavin put his arms around her. He gripped the rifle and pulled it into her shoulder, his face in her hair, smelling the freshness.

"Springtime…" he muttered, his eyes closed, his lips planting a light kiss.

"What? What did you say?" she asked, trying to hold the gun steady.

"Nothing. Hold it like this," he said, nestling the gun into her shoulder and stepping back as soon as he felt her take charge of the rifle. She took aim and fired. And fired. And fired. Five shots later, she hadn't even come close to the target.

"It takes practice. We'll come out again. How's Wednesday afternoon?"

"I have to check my calendar," she said.

"Oh, excuse me! Got so many dates you can't keep track?"

"I have appointments to talk to people about the auction, Mr. Know-it-all."

"Oh, yeah. I forgot."

April turned around to face him, wearing a hurt expression. She stepped closer to him and looked up directly into his clear blue eyes. He started to sweat.

"I don't know why you don't get it…I'm only interested in you, Fireman."

When he didn't answer, she got up on her toes and kissed him lightly. "Thanks for the lesson," she said, turning away and heading home.

Catching up to her, he handed her the .22. "You keep the gun, April. Then you'll have it if you need it."

They walked side-by-side in silence. When they reached the community, Shirley and Hal lounged on their deck drinking coffee. Gavin veered left after polite greetings to the Barons, got in his truck and drove away.

Chapter Twelve

April went on each shooting lesson with a heavy heart. She managed to push aside her disappointment with Gavin's cool behavior and focus on what he was teaching her. But after each lesson she was drained, sad and lonely as she returned to her cabin by herself to go over her notes and make phone calls, finalizing plans for the auction.

By the second week of shooting lessons, April believed Gavin's infatuation had worn off and he no longer cared for her. She gave up being affectionate or even joking with him, instead remaining silent through each lesson.

While her aim improved dramatically with practice, her heart began to break a little more each time. She realized she'd have to return to San Francisco with her parents. What else could she do? With no job in Pine Grove and without Gavin's love, there was no reason to stay. She could never fight her father's strong will unless she could show good reasons not to go back.

The Birches would close down on Columbus Day. She'd have no place to live. Pine Grove had crept into her heart. She found herself enjoying breakfast at The Luncheonette, chatting with Laura Dailey and the other women in town, shopping at the small but well-stocked grocery store and meeting with the important local people, like the bank president and the folks at the Chamber of Commerce.

Maybe Gavin was right. This town isn't so bad. If I go back to San Francisco, my dreams of adventure will die anyway. Maybe Pine Grove is meant to be my adventure.

April was lost in gloomy thoughts when Romeo appeared. It was almost time for her lesson and the feline wasn't supposed to be there yet. He landed on the deck railing but almost fell off. He was limping. April approached him, speaking softly, but when she touched his injured paw, he hissed and swiped at her with his claws, slicing a thin cut on her hand.

"Ouch!" She yanked her hand back quickly and he took off, jumping down on the deck and off into the lane.

April followed him, calling his name, but he remained one jump ahead of her. She continued to the burned-out barn where Gavin rescued a fellow firefighter. Yellow hazard tape still zigzagged across the barn door, indicating danger but Romeo managed to scoot under the tape and enter the rickety barn anyway.

April stopped at the door, peering in. Much of the roof was gone and parts of walls. The loft still stood but didn't appear safe. There was one long, partially charred beam left. Romeo climbed up to get away from her and went out onto the beam, where he sat down and proceeded to lick his injured paw.

She slipped under the tape and entered the barn. It still smelled of smoke and burnt wood. The ladder to the loft was untouched by the fire and appeared to be sturdy enough for her. If she could get up there and grab Romeo, she could bring him down and get him to the vet. The injured cat stopped licking long enough to stretch out his bulk on the beam. He rested for a few moments then went back to licking his fur, ignoring April.

She grabbed the rungs of the ladder to test them. Slowly she rose, step by step as the ladder continued to support her weight. When she reached the loft, there was no hay left and some of the flooring was burned out. She stepped carefully, testing before placing her full weight on each weakened board.

She made it over to the beam with Romeo focused on cleaning his fur. Placing first one knee on the beam, then the other, she slowly crept out onto the heavy wood piece, inching closer and closer to the cat in the middle. As she neared, she heard a loud crack and looked up to see the beam crack at the far end, where it was burned badly. Her weight caused it to separate from the wall. April's eyes widened and she started to back up, but it was too late. The beam broke completely off the far wall. She wrapped her arms and legs around the wood as it began to tilt downward. Gripping harder, she felt splinters dig into her palms and legs.

With an even louder sound, the end behind her gave way. Her weight caused it to rotate and fall, landing April on her back on the floor with the beam on top of her and Romeo anchored on top of the beam, digging his claws into the wood. The fall knocked the wind out of her. She lay there trying to catch her breath but when she did, a stabbing pain on her right side prevented her from inhaling deeply. She gasped at the sharpness with each breath she took. Piercing, stabbing pains kept her from moving. She held her breath to stop the pain. Then she tried to push the beam off her, but it was too heavy for her to budge. She lay there, trying not to cry. Romeo looked at her, licked her hair a couple of times and then scampered off.

April tried to call out but couldn't gather enough breath to make a loud sound. Her chest hurt, her back and head hurt, she felt dizzy. The last sounds she heard were the buzzing of a hummingbird and song of a chickadee before she passed out.

GAVIN WALKED FROM HIS truck, practicing his speech in his head on how this was her last lesson and he wouldn't see her until after the auction. When he got to the deck, she was nowhere to be seen. He sat and waited a while, doing a slow burn.

Just like her to stand me up now.

Then he shook his head. In fact, it was totally unlike April not to be there. She never missed an appointment or a date of any kind. She always showed up and always on time. He looked at his watch, fifteen minutes late...not April's style. He ran his hand through his hair trying to figure out where she could be. Shirley walked onto her deck with a glass of iced tea, and waved, "Hi, Gavin."

"Have you seen April, Shirley? She was supposed to meet me here."

"In fact I did see her, about an hour ago. She was following the cat."

"Romeo?"

"I think it was him. He was well ahead of her, but he was limping."

"Which direction?"

Shirley pointed toward the Henderson's burned out barn and Gavin nodded his thanks. He started off, wondering how far they had gone. After ten minutes, he spotted the charred building in the distance. He could barely make out the orange cat lying down outside it, grooming himself. But no April to be found. One of the strips of yellow tape was flapping in the summer breeze.

The barn isn't safe. Was she stupid enough to go in there?

Panic began to build. His heart thudded in his chest as he ran toward it. When he got to the blackened structure, he was breathing too heavily to call out.

"April! Are you in here?"

Though he didn't hear anything, he busted through the tape anyway, and into the barn. He knelt next to her, pushing a few strands of hair off her face. When she saw him, tears formed.

"Can you talk?" He asked her.

"A little," she whispered.

Gavin slowly moved the heavy beam off her chest. Then he took out his cell phone.

"Don't move a muscle. I'll be right back. I'm going outside to call the ambulance," he said.

"Don't leave me," she whispered.

"I'll only be gone for a minute. I'm coming right back. I won't leave you, I promise. Try not to cry."

The call completed, Gavin returned and sank down next to her.

"Does it hurt when you breathe?"

She nodded.

"Take short shallow breaths. Did you lose consciousness?"

"Once," she whispered.

"Follow my instructions." He took her hand and she squeezed it.

"What are you doing here? It's dangerous."

She motioned to him she couldn't talk. He smiled.

"Sorry. Springtime..." he said, brushing his fingers down her cheek, pushing teardrops aside.

When she heard him say "Springtime", she managed a half grin.

"Don't be afraid. The ambulance'll be here soon."

"Stay with me?" She whispered.

"I'll be with you the whole time. I won't leave you. I promise. Were you chasing after Romeo?" He asked, squeezing her hand gently.

She managed a nod. The faint sounds of a siren grew louder.

"I have to go outside and show them where you are," he explained, letting go of her hand.

He ran outside, waving his arms at the approaching vehicle. The stopped and spoke to the fireman. Gavin wheeled in the gurney as he explained what happened. They placed a blanket on the ground next to April.

"This might hurt a little bit. We're going to slide you onto the blanket then lift the blanket and you up and onto the gurney. We don't know if you have internal injuries, so we don't want to jostle you much," Gavin explained.

April's eyes widened with fear, but she gave a nod and reached for Gavin's hand.

The two EMT's lifted her easily a couple of inches and moved her to the blanket quickly. April grimaced and gasped in pain. Her face paled.

The men lifted the blanket by the corners and set her gently onto the gurney, then they wheeled outside. Gavin got in first and eased her in next to him. He took her hand. When they closed the doors, he leaned over and kissed her lightly on the lips.

"You're going to be okay. We're going to take you to Willow Falls because you need a CT scan and some other things they don't have at the clinic in Oak Bend. It's only thirty miles and we'll go fast. Dr. Barrow, in emergency is a friend of mine. He'll treat you right."

April kissed his hand, then closed her eyes.

"April! Wake up! You must stay awake, okay?"

"Kiss me," she whispered, motioning to her lips.

"I suppose kissing would keep you awake?" He chuckled as he bent over, placing his mouth over hers while the ambulance rode slowly over the uneven ground to the street.

"This is more fun than smelling salts," he said, smiling at her.

She put her hand on his cheek and puckered up again.

GAVIN CALLED SUNNY and Mike, who assured him they were headed to the hospital and then he called Dr. Barrow who was waiting for April when the ambulance arrived. Dr. Barrow shook Gavin's hand while the EMT's pulled her out of the ambulance.

"Now you're in my hands," the doctor said to her.

She clung to Gavin's hand, but the doctor shook his head.

"Is he your husband or fiancé?"

April shook her head.

"Then he can't come in. You have to undress and we need to check you out, April...is it?"

Gavin nodded.

"So he stays out here," Dr. Barrow said.

April started to cry.

"Come on, you're too old for tears," the medical man scoffed.

"I won't leave. I'll stay in the waiting room, I promise," Gavin said, taking her hand.

"Okay," she whispered as the orderlies wheeled her into the emergency room.

"Take good care of her, Doc," Gavin said.

"Your girlfriend, eh?"

Gavin nodded, "Yeah, she is."

Dr. Barrow raised his eyebrows at Gavin. "You've got good taste."

Gavin bit his lip and watched the doctor walk away. The nurse tapped him on the elbow. "I'm going to make a fresh pot of coffee. Come, have a cup. You look like you need it."

He nodded and smiled at her, following into the waiting room. Yep, coffee would have to do while he waited to find out if she'd be all right.

It was a long day by the time all the tests were taken and April was bandaged up and ready to be released. Sunny and Mike stayed until Sunny needed a nap. Laura Dailey showed up.

April, on pain medication, looked drowsy, but able to speak. As she was being wheeled out, Laura pulled Gavin aside.

"She's comin' to stay with us," she informed him.

"What?"

"You heard me. The poor girl has no one. Sunny's pregnant. She can't take care of April and the girl can't live alone in a cabin. I've invited her to stay at our house, in the guest room and she's accepted."

"Aunt Laura...you're crazy!"

"Why? What's wrong? Don't you like her anymore?" his aunt asked, her small, keen eyes boring into him.

"Of course I do, but...but having her there...it's hard enough."

"I imagine it is...and you *will* stay away from her! No hanky-panky in my house. What you do in your apartment is your own business, but in my house...my guest room..."

"Don't worry about it, Aunt Laura. Please! There won't be any of—of...anything going on. Believe me," Gavin said, turning pink.

Aunt Laura pulled up the car when an attendant wheeled April out to the street in a wheelchair. She was woozy from a shot of a powerful pain killer and happy to see Gavin.

"I'm coming to live with you...yippee!" she said, shooting him a loving look.

"Great," he said, gritting his teeth behind a tight smile as he opened the back door.

After he helped her into the car, she threw her arms around his neck and kissed him, thrusting her tongue into his mouth. Gavin, taken by surprise, tried to ease her back down on the seat, but April wasn't cooperating. She clung to him.

"Maybe you better sit in the back, Gavin," Laura chuckled as she put the car in gear.

The hospital attendant shut the door. Gavin fell back when as Laura hit the gas.

Chapter Thirteen

By the time they reached Pine Grove, it was midnight. Barney waited on the front porch. April slept with her head on Gavin's shoulder. She woke up with a stiff neck and pain in her chest. Barney opened the door. Gavin slipped out and extended his hand to April.

"Don't. If you pull, it'll hurt," she said, sliding across the seat slowly and swinging her legs over the side of the car. She stood up on shaky pins. Gavin caught her as she listed to the right. As he held her against him, she closed her eyes, rested her cheek on his chest and took in his piney scent.

"Are you dizzy?" Gavin asked.

She shook her head. "Resting," she said.

"Can I carry you up the stairs, April, hon?" Barney asked.

"I can take care of her," Gavin snapped.

Gavin propped her against him and started to walk her slowly toward the stairs. She put her arm around his waist and leaned into him more than she needed to. He made her feel safe. Gavin supported her elbow as she slowly climbed the stairs, gasping with every step as stabbing pain from her broken ribs shot through her chest.

When they got inside, Aunt Laura disappeared into the kitchen mumbling something about tea.

"So, Miss April. What happened to you?" Barney asked, arranging a set of four matching tea cups and saucers with bright flower designs on the kitchen table. Gavin helped her into her seat. She took out a bottle of pills and measured out two in her hand, setting them next to her empty tea cup.

"I broke two ribs and got a concussion," she explained.

"My! What happened?"

"I was trying to rescue Romeo when the beam gave way."

"She was in the Henderson barn," Gavin added.

"No internal injuries, thank God," Laura said, pouring tea into cups.

"Thank Gavin," April said, preparing to take her medication.

Barney looked at Gavin and smiled. "He knows what he's doing," Barney commented, bringing down a tin of homemade cookies.

When they finished eating, Laura showed April to her room. The guest room was covered in a small flower-print wallpaper with lavender and light green on a white background. There was a double bed with three large pillows on top of a hand-quilted bedspread in a lavender patchwork design. A small pine chest sat at the foot of the bed, and a night stand with a white milk glass lamp on top stood to the right. A small rocker was tucked into one corner of the tidy room. April found her new accommodations quite charming.

But she was exhausted. She was wearing clothes Sunny brought to the hospital since they'd cut her clothes off to examine, test and wind an ace bandage around her. Sunny didn't bring other clothes as she didn't realize April was going to the Dailey's house. Laura brought in one of her nightgowns.

"Just us girls here," Laura said, helping April off with her T-shirt and shorts, "I'll pull it quickly over your head so it won't hurt for long."

April shut her eyes, raised her arms slowly as Laura took the garment off and blushed to be so naked in front of Gavin's aunt. She folded her arms across her chest.

"Don't think you'll be wearing a bra anytime soon," Laura said, looking at the bulky bandages around April's midsection.

Laura handed April the nightgown, but the young girl pushed it aside.

"It's too hot. I'd rather sleep like this."

"Of course, honey. This is your room now. You're free to sleep however you want," Laura said, hiding her surprise.

April got into bed and Laura pulled the sheet up over her. She settled down into the three soft pillows as the pain medication kicked in.

"I can't thank you enough for everything you are doing for me," murmured April.

"Don't be silly, what are friends for?" Laura said, waving her hand.

There was a knock on the door and Gavin entered without waiting for an answer. "Came to say goodnight," he said.

Laura got up, kissed April on the forehead and went out, giving Gavin a cautionary look before she closed the door.

He sat on the edge of the bed and took her hand. April pulled him to her for a kiss.

"April, we can't be doing this..." he said, pulling back from her.

"Touch me," she whispered in his ear, desire racing through her body.

"What? Are you nuts?"

"I want you," she whispered, placing his hand on her breast.

He removed his hand immediately.

"You're loopy on meds, Springtime. You're all bandaged up...and I'm not...not...touching you or anything else in this room," he said, moving to stand up.

"Don't leave," she said, putting her hand on his forearm.

"You need to sleep. And I need to go, seeing as you're not...dressed or anything. I shouldn't even be in here," he said.

"Thank you for saving me," she said, her eyelids growing heavy.

"Anytime, Springtime," he said, bending down to kiss her goodnight.

He turned out the light and closed the door on his way out.

GAVIN WORKED ON THE farm and at the firehouse. He was anxious to stay away from the alluring April. The memory of her firm breast resting in his hand took over his mind. If she continued to come on to him when she was on medication, he wasn't sure how long he could resist. He knew his desire to make love to her was already almost beyond endurance. Best to avoid her rather than put temptation in his path.

At dinner, they sat down together. April, terrible pain in the afternoon, gave up her auction duties to take a nap. Laura fussed over their guest, baking an apple pie and preparing snacks and tea for her whenever she got a break from housework.

Thanks to Sunny, April wore own clothes. No matter what she wore or didn't wear, Gavin thought her the prettiest girl he'd ever seen. Against his will, he was getting used to having her around and it made him damn nervous.

"What all are you doin' for this auction thing?" Barney asked.

"I'm trying to get corporate sponsors...companies to donate money to pay for printing the catalogs of what's to be auctioned off," she explained.

"How many people do you thinkll come?" he asked.

"I don't know. We have thirty-five artists donating artwork. Their stuff'll be displayed first on Friday night...then auctioned off on Saturday. It's become a two-day event. I hope people'll come and stay two nights instead of one, doubling the revenue to the local businesses."

"How many people?"

"Hotel, motel and B & B rooms are filling up. I'd guess maybe, two hundred fifty."

"Sure would help our town." Barney put in.

"Sunny didn't start this to help the community, only for the A.S.P.C.A., but it has grown so big...now it *is* a community event," April said.

"We never went before, but we'll be there this year, right, Gavin?" Barney said.

Gavin smiled his agreement as he shoved a forkful of food in his mouth.

"I wouldn't miss it," Laura said. "Everyone'll be talking about it for months. We gotta see what it's all about."

"Gavin, I was hoping you'd come...as my date," April said, taking a forkful of chicken pot pie.

"Okay," he said, keeping his gaze on his plate.

After dinner, April was exhausted. She excused herself and took a book to bed.

"I'll be right in to help you get ready," Laura announced from the kitchen.

"Sure you wouldn't like me to help you," Gavin whispered in her ear, a wicked grin on his face.

"I thought you weren't talking to me," she said.

"Pretty hard to keep quiet with you living here."

Laura joined them. "Youth..." she muttered under her breath, shaking her head.

She took April by the hand and led her into the guestroom.

"Come, let's get the sheep away from the wolf," said Laura.

April laughed, then immediately doubled over in pain.

"Laura, don't make me laugh," she gasped.

"Well, don't keep inviting the wolf into your barn, sweetie," Laura said, chuckling.

Tossing and turning, unable to sleep, Gavin gazed at the clock *Two thirty!* He shook his head, then yanked down the covers and crept downstairs. He didn't bother with a robe as he expected the rest of the household would be in dreamland.

It was bad enough April had broken his heart and tempted him, almost beyond endurance. But with her in the house, well, he could kiss a good night's sleep goodbye. The idea that she was undressed and in the bed downstairs gave his imagination plenty of ideas. Annoyance gathered in him. What was his aunt thinking, inviting April here? How could she expect a guy to ignore such a beautiful girl only a flight away.

Heading for the kitchen and a glass of warm milk, he spied light from under her door. With a rueful grin, he guessed he hadn't been the only one who couldn't sleep. Later, April rolled over and woke up to pain spiking through her chest. She moaned.

Slowly he opened the door opened. The faint creak of the hinge gave him away. A gasp followed by a moan greeted him as he peeked around the door.

"What are you doing up?" he asked, lounging against the jamb.

"I could ask you the same question."

"You first."

"I rolled over and pain woke me up. My meds wore off. Just took some more. I'm hoping I can get back to sleep soon."

He walked in sat down on the edge of her bed and ran his palm over her pale cheek. She looked up at him, tears welling and spilling over. She leaned against his bare chest and cried. He closed his fingers over her shoulder.

"The pain is wearing me down. I have too much to do before the auction and I can hardly stand the pain," she wailed, reaching for a tissue.

He closed his arms around her gently and stroked her hair, placing tender kisses on her head. She planted her palms against him. She stayed in his arms until she calmed down, resting her cheek against his shoulder, her eyes slowly closing.

"You?" she murmured.

"I couldn't sleep. It's strange knowing you're down here, a staircase away."

"I thought you didn't want to have anything to do with me anymore."

"I don't...ah, I didn't. I don't know. Knowing you're here...messes me up. I can't stop thinking about you, Springtime."

"Can't stop thinking about you either."

Gavin stroked her back covered only in ace bandages as she leaned against him. He closed his eyes drinking in her scent of spring roses. Her breathing became even, he felt her relax, realizing she was asleep. He gently lowered her down on the pillows, then pulled the sheet up, careful to make sure she was covered.

Leaning forward, Gavin kissed her lightly on the lips and wiped the last tears from her cheeks with his thumb before tucking the sheet around her. After turning out the light, he tiptoed out, closing the door quietly behind him and ran smack dab into Aunt Laura.

"Thought I might find you sneaking out of her room," Aunt Laura sniffed."

Gavin started and bumped into a wall. "I wasn't sneaking anywhere. I couldn't sleep…"

"So you naturally ended up in April's room?" his aunt asked, her arms crossed.

"I saw the light under her door. I knew she was up."

"And what were you two up to in there…if I dare ask!"

"Aunt Laura! I'm thirty years old!"

"Old enough to immoral behavior in *my* house!"

The sound of a heavy person on the stairs surprised both Laura and Gavin as Barney thudded down the last step.

"What the heck is going on down here?"

"Barney! What are you doing up?" Laura asked him.

"Rolled over and you were gone."

"I heard Gavin on the stairs and found him creeping out of April's room!"

"Laura! He's a man now. He's thirty. Leave him alone and come back to bed. Goodness sakes, woman! He doesn't need a nosy nanny like you checkin' up on him. Come on, now. Good night, Gavin," Barney said, taking Laura by the arm.

She gave Gavin one last dirty look before she trounced up the stairs. Following behind, Barney shot a knowing smile at his nephew, then disappeared upstairs before Gavin could respond.

He lay down on the sofa in the living room, tucked an afghan around himself, and drifted off. Laura found him there when she got up, feeling cranky from lack of sleep. She left him to sleep while she went in to fix breakfast

"I'LL GO," GAVIN SAID, finishing off the last of his coffee.

Laura, Barney and April sat at the kitchen table with him, finishing breakfast.

"I only need a few things, but they're important. Especially my auction file. I made a list," April said, plucking a paper from the pocket of her robe.

"I won't be long," he said, pushing back his chair.

"Thank you." She smiled.

"I'll tell the pigs you're on an errand of mercy," Barney said.

When Gavin drove over to April's cabin, he was surprised to see two big suitcases on the deck. He approached he noticed a fresh dish of cat food on the deck railing with Romeo happily chomping away.

"Hello?" he called.

Cassie appeared in the doorway. "Gavin! Hi! Where's April?"

"Cassie...you're back! April had an accident, chasing after this guy here. She's staying with my Aunt and Uncle. Long story. Justin'll be happy you're back. Where were you? He expected you up here as soon as you got home from Europe...I mean we all expected it," Gavin said, trying not to reveal Justin's keen interest in Cassie.

She sat down on the bench facing him and colored a little.

"Wasn't sure I was coming back," she admitted.

"Why not?"

"Justin didn't seem...too interested..."

"Are you kidding? He was pounding us all the time, wanting to know where you were."

"Every time I called him late at night, like two o'clock in the morning here, I got his machine...so I assumed after three times...he was...uh...sleeping somewhere else."

"He's a cop, Cassie! Emergencies happen. Besides, he spends a couple of nights a week on night duty. They all do that...rotate nights. You must have called on the wrong night."

"Really?" She said, hope creeping into her voice.

"Are you kidding? He's been a wild man since you left."

"You're not just saying that?" She asked, cocking an eyebrow.

"Driving me nuts." Gavin said, putting his hands on his hips.

Cassie colored as she smiled at Gavin.

"Why did you return if you thought he was seeing someone else?"

"Karen invited me...and I had so much fun...and..." she said turning her gaze away from him.

"Truth, Cassie!" Gavin said, moving in front of her.

"Couldn't walk away without being sure. Justin is so...so...special to me," she said, looking down at her hands.

"He's going to flip when he sees you."

"Yeah?" A big grin spread across her face."

"Yeah. I came here to feed Romeo, but since you're back..."

"I'll take over the cat. Can I see April?"

"Justin first, I'll drive," Gavin said, walking down the steps then waiting for her to accompany him.

When Gavin pulled in, he knew Justin was in the office because the two Sheriff's Department cars were in the parking lot. Cassie jumped out and Gavin waited. Justin came to the window and saw Cassie walking toward the building. He flew out the door and raced over to her, picking her up and swinging her around. Then he smothered her in passionate kisses and Gavin knew it was time to leave. He drove home, anxious to break the news Cassie was back.

When he entered the yellow house, April was sitting on a straight-backed chair talking on the phone. She'd spread out papers on the coffee table, a pen in her hand and a clipboard resting on her lap. When she saw him, she waved and kept talking. He dropped a bag of the things he'd brought from the cabin next to her feet.

"She's been on the phone all day," Laura said. Gavin went to the kitchen for a beer.

"She's working, Aunt Laura." Gavin replied, taking a bottle out of the refrigerator.

"Every minute of every day. She popped those pain pills and got started right after you left this morning."

"Should be a good auction then. I'm sure April knows what she's doing," he said, trying to ignore his aunt.

"I hope you're right," she said, wiping her hands on her apron.

He was using all his self-control to stay away from April while she was living there. He holed up in his apartment with a book most evenings, leaving her to read or watch TV with Laura and Barney.

After everyone was in bed, Gavin tiptoed downstairs and crept into April's room to check on her. Sometimes, he tucked the sheet around her if there was a cool breeze or he pulled the blanket down if it was hot. Then he'd sneak up close and kiss her forehead before returning to his bed. He figured Laura heard him, but she never said a word.

When he returned to the living room, April was off the phone, up and stretching slowly.

"Cassie is back," Gavin announced as he joined her, beer in hand.

"She is? Great! Does Justin know?" April grimaced in pain.

"Dropped her off there before coming home. She fed Romeo." He held the beer up for a gulp.

April's eyes glistened with happy tears. "You were going to feed Romeo?"

"Of course," he said with a quick nod. "Can't let him starve...though he is the one who led you to the barn."

"You're so sweet," said April, slowly crossing to him, taking his face in her hands and planting a kiss on his lips while Laura watched.

"What are you doing?" He asked, moving back from her quickly.

"Giving you a 'thank you' kiss. Not allowed?"

Heat flooded Gavin's face and Laura chuckled.

"A simple 'thank you' is enough," he said, wiping his mouth with the back of his hand.

Barney, watching from the stairs, stomped into the living room. "Youth is wasted…"

"…On the young," Laura said, wiping her hands on the dishtowel tucked into the waistband of her skirt as she walked into the kitchen.

MADISON WAS THE THIRD hospital Juan and Caleb visited. At each one, they inquired about the whereabouts of April Mc-something, the girl from the explosion and each time they were met with blank stares. Juan was running out of patience as he approached the front desk.

"I'm inquiring about a patient who was here a month or two ago."

"Are you family?" the pretty clerk asked him.

"A cousin," he lied.

"Name of the patient," she asked, looking down at her computer keyboard.

"April…uh…Mc-something,"

"She's your cousin and you don't know her name?"

"She just got married and I forgot. She was in an explosion," he explained.

"I remember her," the clerk said, looking down at her computer keyboard.

"Do you have a location?" Juan asked.

"I can't tell you, since you're not related, Mr…."

"Cousin Juan."

She looked at him coldly.

"Sorry," she said, not meaning it and turned away.

Juan returned to the car. "She wouldn't tell me, but she knows where Rusty's girl is. Here," Juan said, handing Caleb a wad of bills.

"What?"

"Take her out to dinner. Get the information."

"I'll get it," Caleb said, pulling a comb out of his pocket and combing his hair in the rearview mirror.

"I want to leave tomorrow."

Caleb nodded and got out of the car. Juan drove away as his partner sauntered into the hospital and up to the information desk.

The next morning, Juan and Caleb were ready hit the road at ten a.m. Caleb threw his suitcase in the trunk of the car and got into the front passenger seat. Juan looked at him with a question in his eyes.

"Pine Grove, New York. I've got a map. Should take us about two hours."

Juan put the car in gear as Caleb unfolded it.

THREE WEEKS BEFORE the auction, April shed her bandages and moved back into her cabin with Cassie, who was out every night with Justin. Sometimes he stayed for dinner. April invited Gavin, but he always gave some excuse. She bounced around like a third wheel with Cassie and Justin always touching each other, giggling and stealing kisses. She missed Gavin, but couldn't find a way to entice him.

Convinced she'd lost him, she wondered if she'd ever had him at all. She thought of him every time she looked at the rifle, resting on the dresser in her bedroom.

Cassie returned to the cabin later and later each night. It wasn't long before she wasn't coming back at all. Within a week, Cassie collected her things and moved in with Justin. April was alone again. Her physical recovery progressed well. She walked, then ran around the lake, building up her strength.

Early one morning, when she arose to run, she heard Romeo. She put out his food and went inside to dress. Before long, she heard a strange, low sound, then Romeo growling and hissing. April peeked out the door to spy the mother black bear on her deck, eating Romeo's food. At first she froze in the doorway. The bear turned to her, uttering a low growl of warning.

April backed into the house and ran for the rifle. With shaking hands she pulled back the bolt and loaded the magazine.

"Rest you finger on the side of the gun, not on the trigger," she repeated to herself.

When the magazine was loaded in, April released the bolt and the safety. With her finger lying next to the trigger, she went back to the door and opened the screen. The bear was still there, licking Romeo's bowl. The cat protested and the bear took a swipe at him. April saw her long claws and gulped. She raised the gun, her arms shaking, took aim to the right of the bear, and fired.

The bear stopped and stared directly at April, who took a breath and fired the gun three more times off to the right, intentionally missing the creature, lumbered off the deck heading toward the woods.

April went out on the deck, the gun still raised but shaking badly, and watched the bear join her cubs, and then lope into the woods and disappear.

April put the safety back on, pointed the gun down and went back into the house. She sank down on the sofa and tears formed. She heard a soft knock on her door and turned to see Hal in the doorway.

"Is everything all right?" he asked, cupping his eyes as he peered inside.

She fairly flew out the door and into his arms, bursting into tears. He held her tight until she calmed down enough to tell him what happened. They sat down on the bench and within a few minutes, April stopped shaking.

"Call Gavin and tell him how well you did," Hal suggested.

"He's not interested."

"Any teacher wants to know when their student succeeds. Call him."

After Hal returned to his cabin, April fixed coffee. She picked up her cell.

"I shot it today," she said.

"You shot who today?" Gavin asked.

"I shot the bear."

"You killed a bear?"

"No, silly. I shot at the bear."

"You shot and missed and the bear didn't attack you?"

"I missed on purpose. I didn't want to kill the bear. She has cubs. She's a mother. I wanted her to go away, so I shot close to her...to the right, so she'd go to the left and leave. I took aim like you taught me, and missed her by about a foot. I fired four shots."

"Why not five?"

"I was saving the last shot in case she charged me."

"Good thinking."

"Thanks. Thanks for teaching me. Thanks for lending me the gun, too."

"She probably won't come back. Maybe you should feed Romeo in the house."

"I will. Thanks for the suggestion."

"April...I..." he started but his voice drifted to silence.

"Gavin?"

"Never mind. See you around," he said and hung up the phone.

Tears stung April's eyes. She didn't understand his distance and she missed his affection. She sighed and sat in the rocking chair, picking up her clipboard and made her to-do list for the day while she rocked to and fro for comfort.

Chapter Fourteen

Gavin had spent the week thinking about April. His guts were tied in a knot as the auction approached and the day after, when he would know if April chose him or Rusty. He stayed away from her because it was too painful to be near her knowing she might not be his. He'd never wanted a woman this badly before and waiting tore him up. He kept himself occupied with extra duty at the firehouse and working night and day on his house. He wanted desperately to finish it. He needed something to offer April if she picked him...or maybe to help her pick him.

Laura and Barney noticed how silent Gavin was at meals and he tumbled into bed early every night, exhausted. Still, they didn't say anything but knitted brows and worried expressions on two older faces became the norm at the breakfast table.

Gavin was grateful his aunt and uncle didn't ask questions. He didn't have any answers anyway. He noticed their silence and looks they exchanged when they thought he wasn't looking. Gavin didn't miss a thing. But he pretended to be oblivious to save himself the embarrassment of revealing the truth to them. After courting April with all his heart, she could easily spurn him for someone else.

By Friday night, worry trumped exhaustion. At three-thirty a.m., Gavin got out of bed, threw on shorts, grabbed his binoculars and headed for the firehouse. Maybe he'd be early enough to catch a glimpse of the pair of eagles. *At least someone has a mate.*

He slipped out quietly, wondering if he was silent enough not to wake Laura, who possessed sensitive ears, and doubted he had been.

Pine Grove was quieter than ever, even the birds were asleep. Gavin climbed the stairs and stared at the moonlight reflecting off the lake. The water was so still it looked like dark glass and the full moon shone its light down like a bright beacon, bouncing off and illuminating the pine and oak trees. Gavin marveled at the beauty of the night. But then a sound cut through the silence, a crunch, then another, then another. He turned and saw the figure of a woman walking on gravel approaching the firehouse. It was April.

As she got closer, his heart began to pound. Never an insecure lad who couldn't make up his mind, Gavin didn't know what he'd say to her or what she was coming to say to him. Would she smash his heart to pieces by telling him she'd made plans to return to the dead guy? He said a quick prayer, hoping that wasn't going to happen.

As she approached the firehouse, his mind raced, anticipating what she had in her heart. He watched her climb the ladder and swing her legs over the short wall. They stood facing each other, silently. April moved closer and he didn't back away. Time to face the truth, be it good or bad.

"It's almost time for the auction," she said.

"I know." He faced her squarely.

"And after…after that…I have to make a decision." She looked down at her hands.

"Rusty or me."

She shook her head. "I have to choose between staying in Pine Grove or going back to San Francisco with my parents."

"What about Rusty?"

"I told you, he's not an option."

"Oh? Did he tell you not to join him?"

"I haven't heard from Rusty. He's not an option because I don't want him. Why won't you believe me?"

"Don't forget, I saw you two together." Gavin didn't move but continued to stare into her eyes.

"There's no other way to say it," she said.

"Go ahead then. Say what you came to say." He put his hands on his hips, wishing he could slow down his racing heart.

"I'll have to be blunt."

He nodded, bracing himself for bad news.

"I love you, Gavin," she said, a rosy blush colored her cheeks.

Silence filled the air.

"What?" His heart beat so loudly in his ears, he wasn't sure he heard right.

"You heard me. Do I have to say it again? Okay. I love you."

"You do?"

She nodded. "I want to stay in Pine Grove. You were right about this town...it grows on you."

"You want to stay here with me...forever?" he asked, cocking an eyebrow.

"How can I convince you?"

She turned and walked to the far end of the firehouse, the side facing the lake and looked up. The moonlight followed them every evening they'd been together, beaming down its glow. He watched it dance on the lake. The eagles flew by as the night waned. The moon threw out its final brilliance. Gavin followed coming up right behind her and put his hands on her shoulders.

"One kiss in the moonlight," she said.

He cocked an eyebrow. "One kiss?"

"All it should take to convince you, one kiss in the moonlight," she said, turning to face him.

She reached up and slid her hands up his chest, folding them together behind his neck, pulling him down to her. April brought her chin up as his head came down and their lips met.

Slowly, gently at first, she kissed him, nibbling on his lower lip. Then he took over as passion grew. He ran the tip of his tongue over her lips then eased it into her mouth.

Their tongues danced. Gavin angled his head to deepen the kiss as he crushed her April melted into his body, softening against him, welcoming him. Gavin held her close as his tongue took possession of her mouth. He had missed her, touching her, kissing her and drank deeply at her lips, greedy for the taste and scent of her.

His hands slid up and down her back, holding her close. His fingers slipped under the back of her T-shirt to feel her silky skin. Touching her increased his desire and he tightened his grip slightly. He wanted to continue. Time stopped for Gavin as he lost himself in their embrace. But April finally pulled away.

"Well?" She asked, trying to steady her breath.

"Well, what?"

"Believe me?"

"I love you, too, April," he said softly.

She smiled up at him, her eyes glistening. Gavin brushed her hair from her forehead as the eagles circled the lake looking for a fish breakfast and daylight cracked through the horizon, sending shafts of soft red mixed with bright sunlight.

April stayed in his arms resting her head on his chest as he pointed to the eagles. Happiness washed over him at the feel of her in his arms. She nuzzled into his chest and Gavin's fingers got lost in her hair. He rested his cheek on her head. Not one to be taken in or fooled by fancy words, Gavin knew kisses didn't lie. He'd won her after all. She would be his at last.

When she looked up at him again, he brought his mouth down on hers in hungry possession again. This time he released the urgency he'd felt for a long time...passion built as desire, want and need blended together to make the would-be lovers cling to each other. April's knees buckled and she leaned heavily against him.

The fire alarm bell cut through the dawn air with one sharp ring, and they jumped apart. Only one ring of the bell, unusual. Gavin looked up then down on the street to see three firefighters doubled over with laughter, watching them. April covered her mouth with her hand as her face turned bright red, matching the color Gavin sensed in his own face. She laughed, and alternated between glancing at the men on the street and Gavin.

"Get a room!" called out Joe, the older of the three men.

His remark renewed their glee and the men convulsed again as they opened up the firehouse for the new day.

"You coming along...or, ah..." asked Joe.

Gavin waved at his coworker. "See you later," he said to April, sliding his palm across her cheek.

"Still my date for the auction?"

"Wouldn't miss it, Springtime," he said, climbing down the ladder.

THOUGH THE AUCTION was two weeks away, Martin and Barbara McKenna decided to give April a surprise by arriving early. Sunny called to tell her they had arrived.

"What? They're here? Already?" April anxiously chewed a cuticle.

"They're staying with us."

"Thank goodness. I don't want them here. I have too much to do."

"Only little details left, right?"

"Details, yes, but a million of them!"

"It'll be okay, April. The art is going to start arriving this week. Can Gavin help Mike haul it to the school? We can store it there."

"I'll ask. When do I have to see them?" She suppressed a groan, aware of how ungracious she sounded.

"Meet us at Homer's for dinner tonight at six."

"Thanks for keeping them occupied until then,"

"No problem. Relax. This is going to be fine."

"You don't know my father," April said, then ended the call.

She fussed about, trying to work but being distracted by having to face her parents. She wasn't anxious to see them. Although she'd thought she had sorted out her life, she knew her father wouldn't agree.

At five-thirty, she put on a red sundress, fluffed her loose curls and headed towards Homer's, hoping for a pleasant meal.

Sunny and Mike sat with Barbara and Martin McKenna at a table for six by the window. Mike was pointing out the most popular fishing spots in the lake when April entered the room.

Sunny spotted her and stood up. The two women embraced, and Sunny whispered, "You look beautiful…radiant, as only a woman in love can look."

April's eyes widened, but before she could speak, Barbara grabbed her daughter for a long hug. Then April's father kissed her on the cheek before he smiled and sat down.

"You look fabulous," Barbara said to her daughter.

"I concur. This country air agrees with you," Martin said.

"Farms boys, too," Mike mumbled.

"What?" Martin said, turning to Mike.

"Nothing, nothing," he said, lowering his gaze after he smiled at April.

"Well, my dear, I hope you will be packed and ready to join us on a car trip through New England, and then of course, you'll be driving back to San Francisco with us."

"Dad, about San Francisco…" April began, chewing her lip.

Martin continued speaking, ignoring her as usual. "I had a devil of a time getting them to hold the internship open for you, but fortunately they did—"

"Dad…I wouldn't hold my—"

"Martin! Do we have to talk about it now?" Barbara asked, knitting her brows.

"Why not, Barbara?"

"We haven't seen our daughter for such a long time. I want to catch up...find out how her life has been—"

"You mean ask about Russell," Martin said, a frown on his face.

"Rusty?" April asked, a tone of surprise in her voice.

"Whatever his name was. I don't want to know about him...lowlife, living with you without marriage."

"Dad, please. I'm not a baby." April rolled her eyes.

"I know about men...only out to get one thing."

"Rusty supported us, Dad. He paid all the bills."

"It's like that with every man. I'm a man, I should know."

"Martin, stop, please," begged Barbara.

"All right, but I don't approve of him and never will," he said, setting his jaw firmly.

"He's gone, Dad."

"And have you replaced him? I understand from Sunny there is a new man in your life. Don't waste any time do you?" A frown cut across his face.

April's face warmed.

"Martin!" Barbara snapped.

"All right. It's none of my business anyway, I suppose. I hope this one's better than the last. Honestly, April! You had Brian, what a great guy, and you let him get away."

April could feel tears of anger pricking at the back of her eyes. Sunny stared at her while Mike buried his face in the menu.

"Gavin is a great guy," Sunny ventured.

April shot her a look but it was too late. "Gavin is it? And what does he do?"

April groaned. "Why don't we order," she said, changing the subject.

"That bad, huh? I'm disappointed," Martin said. "It's a good thing you're coming back to San Francisco." Martin ended the topic by picking up a menu.

"Don't count on it. I'll have the blue cheese burger, Mike's favorite."

"What?" Martin asked.

"I don't want to discuss it now, Dad. We're out to dinner with Sunny and Mike. Let's talk about something pleasant. Did you know Sunny is pregnant?"

"Congratulations," Barbara said, taking Sunny's hand.

"We're pretty happy about it," Mike said, giving his wife a loving look as he slipped his arm around her.

"Have you picked names, Sunny?" Barbara asked.

Sunny shook her head. "It's too new. April has been a big help with our art auction."

"I heard something about that. What is this charity thing you're doing?" Martin asked.

"It's not just a charity event, Martin, though it started out to be. April built it up to be a big community event...driving business for our local..."

"Yeah, yeah, for the local people, the little people. Now in San Francisco..."

"Dad, let Sunny finish!"

"Sorry, sorry. Go ahead," Martin said, a slight color appearing in his cheeks.

"April is getting the local business community involved. This is going to be the biggest event in our county all year. And she's running the show."

"I'm proud of you, dear," Barbara said, a big smile lighting up her face.

April smiled back at her mother.

"Easy to do in a small town, but bring something like that to San Francisco and you'd have to have professionals handling things," Martin said.

April looked down at her hands. Warmth crept into her cheeks.

"A lot of people in this town think very highly of April," Mike put in," When she was injured in her fall in the barn, the whole community turned out to support her."

"What fall? What barn?" Martin sat up straight and glared at April as though he'd just caught her in a heinous lie. "Barbara, is there something you're not telling me?"

Before Barbara could answer, Gavin walked in.

"I thought I'd find you here. Saw Mike's SUV out front. Alice Green from A.S.P.C.A. is looking for you. She's got a shipment of artwork," Gavin strode over to April as he spoke.

He stopped and looked around, then looked at April, who was wishing she could slide under the table. Then he walked over to Barbara McKenna and held out his hand.

"Hi, I'm Gavin Dailey. And you are?"

"Barbara McKenna. This is my husband, Martin," she said.

"Gavin, huh? Are you the Gavin who's shacking up with my daughter?"

Gavin reeled back a half step in surprise. "I beg your pardon?" he asked.

"You heard me," Martin insisted.

"I'm not shacking up with anyone...if it's any of your business. If you mean am I *dating* your daughter, yes, I am."

April looked at him and smiled.

"What do you do for a living?"

"I'm a firefighter and a carpenter."

"Oh boy," Martin said, looking down.

"Gavin, let's talk outside," April said, taking him by the arm and moving him quickly out the front door.

"Your *father?*" He asked in disbelief when they were out of earshot.

She nodded and looked down. "He's a piece of work. Now maybe you can see how I ended up with Rusty."

"I'm not afraid of him."

"I noticed," she said, smiling at him with pride.

"I get why you don't want to go back to San Francisco." His brow knitted into a frown. "You're not using me to get away from him, are you?"

"Why can't you believe I love you?"

He smiled sheepishly. "I do, Springtime, I do. Forget what I said." He pulled her closer. "Will we get some time alone tonight?" He whispered in her ear while nuzzling her neck.

"Doesn't look like it with my parents here," she said with a sigh.

She raised her lips to receive his kiss before he returned to his truck and drove off. April called Alice Green, arranged to have the artwork delivered to the school and rejoined her dinner party.

As they left Homer's, they passed two men, one tall and blond, the other short and dark, strangers in town, who went into Homer's, looking for dinner and a few beers.

LAURA AND BARNEY SMILED at each other across the dinner table while listening to Gavin chatter away.

"Glad to have you back, son," Laura said, looking at him while raising her fork.

"Glad to be back," he responded, cutting a piece of steak. "I met April's parents today."

"Her parents are here, in Pine Grove? Must be here for the auction."

"They're staying with Sunny and Mike, I think."

"Barney, we should have them to dinner."

Gavin hesitated. "I don't know, Aunt Laura. Her dad is a real buster, a tough guy," Gavin said, piling more potatoes on his plate.

"Still, it's the proper thing to do."

"Why?" Gavin asked.

"She being your girl again and all…it's just polite," Laura said, blushing slightly.

Gavin looked at her and grinned. Couldn't fool Laura Dailey about anything.

"If you want to but don't do it on my account," Gavin said.

After dinner, Gavin returned to his apartment. Laura and Barney settled in front of the television set to watch their favorite programs.

It was about ten o'clock when Laura beckoned her nephew down from his apartment. She made tea and broke out some of her special date nut cookies, Gavin's favorites. As they sat eating and drinking, Laura took a deep breath.

"You know I don't tell you what to do…most of the time. Right?"

He nodded. I'm not telling you anything now. I'm doing something I meant to do but keep forgetting with everything going on around here, I'm surprised I can remember my name. Still. It's time. Do you remember your grandma, Gavin?"

"You mean Barney's mother, Nana?"

"I do. She was a great baker…made the best bread and cakes."

"Oh, yes. She had a red velvet cake that melted in your mouth. Thinking about it makes me hungry," Laura said, taking another cookie.

"What about her?"

"She died about fifteen years ago. I think your daddy got some of her things and a little money in her will."

"And…" Gavin prompted.

"We got this," Laura said, producing a small box she placed on the table.

Gavin looked at the box then at his aunt.

"Your grandmother was married to your grandfather happily for fifty years," Laura said, tears coming to her eyes.

Gavin drank some tea and took another cookie while waiting for his aunt to continue.

"Since we don't have our son, Joe, anymore...and we feel like you are our son, we want to give this to you," she said, pausing then going on quickly. "It's not a suggestion or even a hint...something we want to pass on to you before we forget. In case... in case you might have a need for it anytime soon."

She wiped her hands on her apron then opened the box to reveal a stunning ring with a diamond in the center, a ruby on either side and tiny diamonds all the way around.

"This was her engagement ring. Should you ever...decide. If you want to get married...sometime in the future, well, um, Barney and I want you to have this. We hope your future bride...whoever she may be, will like it," she said, handing the box to Gavin.

He picked it up and looked it over, the diamond caught the lights and shone with an inner beauty, taking his breath away.

"It's beautiful, Aunt Laura. I don't know what to say...thank you. It's...absolutely amazing. I'm sure...whoever...I give it to will love it, too. Thank you so much," he said, rising from his chair and leaning over to give his aunt a kiss on the cheek and a hug.

She blushed and smiled at him. "I'm glad you like it, son. So glad."

Gavin stared at the ring and heat came to his cheeks. It was perfect and, as usual, Aunt Laura's timing was spot on. He closed the box, put it in his pocket and finished the cookie and his tea. He rose and looked at the clock. Eleven. He was on for the early morning shift at the firehouse tomorrow. Time to pack it in.

"Good night, Aunt Laura. Tell Barney 'thank you', too," he said.

"Tell me yourself," Barney said, walking into the kitchen.

"Hey, Uncle Barney. It's great, man. I mean. Uh, thank you," Gavin said, shaking Barney's hand.

Barney pulled him into a brief hug and smiled at the young man. "Go get her, son," he whispered.

Gavin grinned then headed for the stairs.

Laura wiped her eyes on her apron.

"Looks like our family will be growing again," Barney said.

"Finally!" She responded, gathering up the tea things and heading to the sink.

From where he'd paused on the bottom step, Gavin grinned.

ACROSS TOWN, THE TALL blond man, Caleb, and the shorter darker man, Juan, walked into the fresh summer air after leaving Homer's. They got in their car and drove to Copley's Cabins on Vine Street.

"Tomorrow we search this stinkin' town for Rusty's squeeze," Juan said. "April."

"Yeah," Caleb chuckled. "How many girls can have a name like hers in this tiny place?"

"Not many. We'll find her."

"Guy said we could have the room until Friday. Said he's sold out Friday night and Saturday. So we gotta find her by then 'cause everything else in this hick town is also sold out."

"If we have to sleep in the car for a night, we will. I ain't approaching her unless everything's right. We gotta get the money," Juan said.

"Whatever. You got a joint? Turn on the tube," Caleb said, pulling out matches.

Chapter Fifteen

April agreed to meet her parents for breakfast at The Luncheonette in the morning. She was encouraged when she looked through the glass door and saw her father smiling.

"Good morning, dear," Barbara said, rising.

April kissed each of her parents then sat down next to her mother.

"April, we need to talk about your coming home," her father began.

Before April could answer, Laura and Barney Dailey walked through the door and waved to April.

"Who are they?" Barbara asked her daughter.

"Gavin's aunt and uncle," April said, her heart sinking as the pair walked over to their table.

She made introductions.

"Won't you join us?" Barbara offered.

April wanted to run away but was trapped sitting in the corner.

"We'd love to, how nice," Laura said, sitting down next to Barbara.

"Thank you for taking care of April when she was injured," Barbara said, patting Laura's arm.

"We were happy to have her. She was no bother at all," Laura replied.

"Some stupid cat got her into a jam," Martin said.

"Romeo is not stupid. He was hurt, Dad," April said.

"Romeo? You named the cat Romeo?"

April blushed and averted her gaze.

Her father laughed. "Sure...you've dated enough Romeos in your life, why not one more," he said.

"Martin!" Barbara barked at him.

"What are you implying?" Barney asked, his face clouding over.

"Nothing, nothing. My daughter seems to attract the love 'em and leave 'em type."

"Are you suggesting my nephew is...is that type of man, too? That he's playing her for a fool?" Laura Daily asked, narrowing her eyes.

"Is he? You know him better than I do."

"Martin!" Barbara gasped, putting her hand on his forearm and squeezing.

"Dad!" April's cheeks colored and her brows drew together.

"April doesn't have any complaints." Barney sniffed.

"Dad, you're embarrassing me. Please, stop," she said, her face burning, her voice rising.

Everyone fell silent and looked at the menu. Dora, the waitress, took their orders and left, coming back almost immediately with a pot of fresh, hot coffee.

"We met your nephew, yesterday. He certainly is a handsome young man," Barbara said.

"He's not so young. He's thirty," Barney said, shortly.

"I only meant..."

"I know. Thank you. Yes, he's a looker," Laura said, smiling.

"He's lucky to be dating April. She graduated cum laude from Wellington College. Just got her MBA from Kensington State. She's smart. She's coming back to San Francisco to start a great internship in my firm," Martin announced.

Laura's face fell. Barney looked at his wife with a quizzical expression.

"Not true!" snapped April. "Please, Laura, Barney...Dad, why did...it's not true."

"Of course it's true. What else are you going to do? Have you got a job here?"

"It doesn't matter. I'm not going back with you."

"April…" Laura said, her hand covering the younger woman's. "Say you're staying."

"I like it here!" April banged her water glass on the table by accident, spilling some, which she quickly wiped up with a napkin.

"How are you going to support yourself here? I'm not going to send you a cent if you stay here." Martin's eyes flashed. He slammed his palm down on the table for emphasis.

"I'll get a job," she said, jutting her chin out slightly.

"Doing what? How many MBA's do you think they need in Pine Grove?" Martin turned his stare on his daughter as he leaned forward in his chair.

"Martin…enough," Barbara said, pulling him back.

"It's true. She knows it, too. Look at her face," Martin said, staring at his daughter.

April felt the sting of tears at the back of her eyes.

"She can always stay with us," Barney piped up.

"Right, "Laura said with a single sharp nod of her head.

The door opened and Gavin stepped through. He saw them sitting together and his brows knit immediately, especially when his gaze stopped on April's face. He was scowling as he marched over to the table.

"Good morning," Gavin said tightly, leaning over to kiss April, "howdy, all."

"Howdy? Spoken like a true country boy," Martin said, laughing.

Gavin's eyes clouded over in anger.

April burst into tears, pushed her chair back, got up, squeezed between her mother's chair and the wall and left."

"Martin, how could you?" Barbara asked and followed her daughter.

"You have a wonderful daughter, Mr. McKenna. I don't understand why you treat her the way you do," Gavin said before following April outside.

Barbara put her arms around April, who rested her head on her mother's shoulder. She tried to hide the tears streaming down her cheeks. When she saw Gavin come outside, April pushed her mother aside gently and moved to him. He put his arm around her shoulders and brushed the last tear from her cheek with his thumb. She put her arm around his waist. Barbara looked at them, and smiled.

"Your father always says the wrong thing, April, you know. He loves you. He only wants the best for you."

"Gavin *is* best for me. It's about time you both stopped questioning my decisions." She raised her chin to emphasize her determination.

April stiffened. Her mother sighed and opened the door.

"You're right. Hard for us, I guess...you're so grown up," she sighed and went back inside to join April's father.

"I hate leaving you with them," Gavin said, pushing a strand of hair from her eyes.

"I'll be okay. Been dealing with him all my life."

"Not for much longer."

She shot him a questioning glance. He lowered his head, gazing at the ground then looked up and grinned at her.

"You're my girl, remember?"

She smiled at him and stepped closer, raising her chin. Gavin took the hint and kissed her, then kissed her again before leaving to return to the firehouse.

April stepped back inside The Luncheonette.

"I have so much to do before the auction, I need to get back home to work," she said, standing next to the table.

"Please stay and have breakfast first. I'm sorry if I said the wrong thing. You know how I am sometimes," Martin said, as he stood and held a chair out for her.

"I am hungry," she admitted, staring at the plate of bacon and eggs.

April sat down and tucked into her food.

"This auction is going to be a big deal," Barney said.

"People...artists...dealers...buyers are coming from New York City to this auction. It's the biggest thing in the county," April said.

Martin opened his mouth to speak, but Barbara put her hand on his arm. He stopped and focused on his food, smiling at his daughter.

"We're going, too," Laura piped up.

"Everyone is going to be there. You going?" Barney asked, shifting to look at Barbara, instead of Martin.

"Of course, we wouldn't miss it," Martin answered for her. He sipped his coffee.

BY NINE O'CLOCK, THE Daileys and McKennas had finished their breakfast and departed before Juan and Caleb sauntered in and sat at a table by the window.

"Get friendly with the waitress, Caleb. She probably knows everyone in this hick town," Juan said.

Dora came over to the table.

"Coffee?" she asked, the big pot hovering over Juan's cup.

"Only if you come with it," Caleb said, his eyes giving her the once over.

She rolled her eyes and forced a smile. "Sorry, boys, only coffee this morning. Know what you want to eat?"

"Is that a leading question?" Caleb said, smirking.

Dora tapped her foot. "I'll come back when you're ready."

"Hey, forget my friend. He's crude sometimes. We're ready," Juan said, kicking Caleb under the table.

They placed their orders and Dora left immediately afterward.

"What's the matter with you, man?" Juan said, flashing angry eyes at his cohort.

"What? You said to come on to her, so I did," answered Caleb, putting sugar in his coffee.

"Not so obvious, idiot! Be nice! Don't you know how to be nice to a woman?"

"What for? They're only good for one thing...maybe two if she's a good cook. Might as well find out right away if she's gonna give it to ya," Caleb said.

"We're not here to do her. We're here to find Rusty's girl. We need *information* from her, not her body."

"Speak for yourself. She isn't bad. I'd take her, easy," Caleb said, his gaze following Dora as she made the rounds of tables lugging the coffee pot.

"Do you want the money or not?"

"Of course I want the money!"

"Then shut up and let me talk. Here she comes with our food."

Dora walked over, the smile falling from her face when she looked at Caleb. She put down two plates, one loaded with pancakes and one with bacon and eggs over easy.

"Here's your breakfast. I'll be right back with your toast."

"Say, say...do you have a minute, Miss...Miss," Juan said.

"Dora. Sure, I guess. What can I do for you?"

"Something big happening in this town this weekend, eh?"

"The art auction is happening. It's a charity event for the animal shelter. Gonna be a ton of people in our little town. Are you going to be here?"

"We weren't planning on it, but maybe, if it's going to be as great as you say."

"Sure is."

"We're here to look up a friend...a friend of a friend. A girl, woman...young woman. Her name is April McKenna. Know her?'

"April McKenna? Of course I know her."

"Great," Juan said, taking another sip of his coffee.

"What do you want with her?" Dora asked, her eyes narrowing.

"Our friend asked us to deliver a package to her. He bought her some jewelry and he's too shy to give it to her directly. Do you know where she lives?"

Dora's suspicion eased a bit. "Yeah. In The Birches. It's a summer community, right up the street. See that road, go up there and take the first left. Go all the way until you can't go any farther."

"Thanks a lot, honey," Juan said, smiling.

Dora delivered the toast and refreshed their coffee.

"Like taking candy from a baby," Juan said, stuffing bacon in his mouth.

"Yeah. Good. Still like that chick," Caleb said, his gaze following the sway of Dora's hips.

"Later, pal, later. Finish up. We've got to check this place out," Juan said, gulping the last of his coffee.

He left a big tip, then put his car in geared and headed for The Birches.

"There are so many cabins here, how are we going to find this chick?" Caleb asked.

"I don't know. Shut up and keep your eyes open," Juan said.

Trying to blend in, the two men kept to the back road, stopping every so often to watch people grilling on their decks or pushing their children in swings. The two men rounded the pool and peeked in, checking out the swimmers, readers and sunbathers.

"Oooh. There are some hot chicks here. I'd like to do her, the one in the red suit...man, look at those..."

"Caleb! Shut up! Do you see any women *without* men?"

"No, but I'm looking."

"Not for you, idiot!"

"I know you mean April McKenna. Why don't we ask someone?"

"Because they will remember us and in case we have to get a little rough with this chick to get the money, I don't want anyone to see us. Get it?"

"Yeah, I get it. All work and no play makes for a...frustrated guy over here. When are we going to find some chicks, Juan?"

"After we get the money. Then you can have any chick you want, okay?"

"I suppose. But I'd be able to concentrate better if I didn't have chicks on my mind."

"It wouldn't matter how many chicks you had, Caleb, you'd always have chicks on your mind," Juan snickered.

"You're right. What else is there, man?"

The two men continued to wander slowly. Juan wasn't sure about the people at the pool. There were several young women there who could have been April McKenna. They continued on to the back parking lot when Juan spied her. She was sitting alone, looking melancholy, petting a cat.

"Gotta be her," Juan said.

"Where?"

"Over there," Juan said, motioning with his head.

Caleb nodded. "We can't just walk up there, Juan. We've got to get her alone," Caleb said, looking around.

"Let's get outta here," Juan said, "we'll have to come back at night, when things are quiet and it's dark."

The two men walked slowly back to the front of the community and out to the street.

APRIL'S MIND WAS ON her troubles, a million miles away from activity in the community. Romeo gave one last purr, then a meow, and was off.

"Ready, April?" called her father.

She glanced up to see her dad striding down the hill toward the cabin. She grabbed a small purse and walked down the steps to meet him. "Hi, Dad."

"I'm looking forward to this dinner," said Martin, avoid muddy patches. "I hear Laura Dailey is a good cook."

April smiled at him. "She is. Are you going to behave?"

"I always behave. I promise to be my most charming self tonight. Don't want to insult a great cook, do I?" he said, smiling.

April stood at the front door, her heart pounding as her father rang the bell. Barney opened the door and ushered them into the cozy living room, where a pitcher of margaritas was waiting.

"Nice house," Martin said, plopping his bulk down in Barney's favorite chair. He scooped up some of Laura's home-made spinach dip on a cracker and put his feet up on a footstool. April cringed, hoping Barney wouldn't mind.

Laura entered the room balancing a bowl of fresh veggies and olives with a plate of cheese and crackers. She placed them on the coffee table, next to the other hors d'oeuvres. Barbara and Martin helped themselves. April's stomach was too queasy for food, but she downed a margarita quickly and asked Barney for another.

Gavin joined them, wearing a freshly ironed, short-sleeved button-down shirt in a shade of blue that matched his eyes. His khaki slacks were pressed with a perfect crease. April blinked at this new version of her man. He lounged on the sofa arm, next to her.

April smoothed a hand over the skirt of her white cotton piqué sundress with a low, heart-shaped neckline. She reached up to check the red ribbon she'd tied in her hair, making certain it was still straight, then she adjusted the gold heart on the chain around her neck. Her parents gave her the necklace on her last birthday and she'd chosen to wear it with the hope of pleasing her father.

Gavin whispered in her ear. "Relax. You look beautiful, Springtime."

She smiled up at the man she loved, and then caught her father staring at them out of the corner of her eye. Peeking into the dining room, she spied the table set with the Dailey's best china. This was the set Laura kept in the corner cabinet, a place of honor, she'd discovered when she'd stayed with them.

After about fifteen minutes, Laura invited them into the dining room. She sat Barbara and Martin together. Barbara and April helped Laura clear the food from the living room.

Stopping at the door, the young woman overheard the kitchen conversation. Barbara remarked to Laura, "They make a handsome couple, don't you think?"

Laura replied, "We're very fond of your daughter, Barbara. We'd be real pleased if Gavin made it permanent with her."

"Me, too. April seems very happy with Gavin."

April entered the kitchen, interrupting the conversation before they started planning her wedding.

"Here you go, dear." Laura handed her a basket of rolls. "Will you carry this in?"

April strolled in just in time to catch some of the conversation among the men.

Martin turned to Gavin. "So, Gavin, what are your plans for the future?"

The fireman shifted in his seat. "I plan to stay with the fire department. It's a good job with benefits. I'm building my own house and plan to farm some."

"You have land?" Martin asked. His eyebrows raised as he looked at Gavin.

"Two acres. My house is almost finished."

"You're building it yourself? Can't afford a contractor?" Martin took a final sip of his margarita.

"I'd rather do it myself. I make it perfect. It's a log home," Gavin said, clenching his fists at his sides.

"You want to put my daughter in a log cabin...like Abe Lincoln?" A cold smile curled Martin's lips.

"My nephew never said anything about putting April in his house, Martin. You're jumping the gun a little, don't you think?" Barney responded.

"Does it have running water, a bathroom?" Martin said, ignoring Barney.

"We're not primitive, Mr. McKenna. Of course it has a bathroom, two in fact," Gavin said, snapping a long piece of celery in half then in half again.

"I think April would be more comfortable in a townhouse in San Francisco…"

"Married to an investment banker?" Gavin inquired, cocking an eyebrow at Martin.

"Why not? Sounds good to me," Martin said, sitting back, lacing his fingers behind his head.

"Don't you think that's her decision?" Gavin asked.

"What does she know? She's twenty-six. Besides, her taste in men…" Martin replied, shaking his head.

Gavin narrowed his eyes and hesitated. April saw the signs that his temper was boiling up inside. Before he could respond, the women came in carrying aromatic platters of barbecued chicken, homemade cole slaw, potato salad, green salad, mango chutney for the chicken and steaming corn on the cob. April blew out a breath.

Martin's attention was drawn to the food and he dropped his questions as he began eating. A hush fell on the room as all mouths were busy consuming food. There were occasional 'ums' and 'ahs' which put a smile on Laura's face but discussion stopped.

Barney looked at April and winked, which made her nervous. She wondered what her father had said while she was out of the room. Gavin looked too steamed to muster up much of a grin. April concentrated on her food and prayed the meal would be over soon.

"Best meal I've eaten in a long time, Laura. You're an excellent cook," Martin said, wiping his chin with his napkin.

"Thank you."

"I must get your recipe for potato salad, Laura." Barbara said, before taking a drink of water.

"Barney makes the potato salad, you'll have to ask him."

"Be happy to write it down for you, Barbara," Barney said.

Barney and Gavin got up to clear the table while Laura brought out her masterpiece, a warm homemade peach pie with French vanilla ice cream. Barbara and April took over serving coffee and tea while Laura dished out the dessert. She gave an extra big piece to Martin, whose eyes had grown wide at the appearance of the confection.

"Laura, I don't know when I've last eaten peach pie...and it's my favorite," he said.

"Glad you like it, Martin. It's my favorite, too," she confided.

Again, like an answer to April's prayers, the room fell silent while everyone ate. She was relieved to see her father smiling but puzzled by the sour expression on Gavin's face. Her stomach sank as she figured her dad must have said something to ruin Gavin's even disposition.

He avoided looking at her, too, another bad sign. *What's going on in your mind, Gavin?* But of course, she couldn't ask the question out loud.

The rest of the evening passed without incident. Barbara put her hand on Martin's arm when his conversation started to veer off course and he stopped and quieted down. At eight o'clock, April suggested it was time to go to The Roadhouse. Laura and Barney begged off as there was so much to clean up.

Gavin sidled up to April, "If I don't go, Al will move in on you," he chuckled.

Martin turned to April.

"We'll be waiting in the car, April," he said.

"I'm riding with Gavin."

Martin looked at her, his brows knitted. "You'll ride with your parents."

"I'm an adult, Dad. I ride where I choose," she said, taking Gavin's hand.

Martin was nonplussed but Barbara moved in on him and steered him toward the Daileys to thank them and say "good night" before she led him out the door. Gavin waited for the McKenna's to get ready so they could follow him to The Roadhouse.

April was silent in the car, as she didn't want to know what her father had said and didn't want to fight with Gavin. He kept his eyes on the road and his thoughts to himself. About halfway there, April couldn't stand it anymore and reached over and took his right hand in hers.

"I love you," she whispered.

He looked over and smiled at her, then he slowed the truck down.

BACK IN THEIR MOTEL room, Caleb couldn't sit still. He paced like a caged animal. "How much longer are we going to sit around, Juan?"

"As long as it takes, my friend." Juan sat back in front of the air conditioner turning the pages of the newspaper. "Hmmm. Live music tonight."

"Where? Live music means girls...women, right?"

"Maybe." Juan shrugged. "A place called The Roadhouse."

Caleb stuffed his wallet in his back pocket and walked to the door. "Let's go."

Juan folded up the newspaper and grabbed the car keys. Caleb read the directions to The Roadhouse.

"If there's music and booze, there will be women," Juan said, making a right turn.

"And where there's women, there's me," Caleb chimed in.

They found a parking space at the back of the lot because the rest were taken. After getting beer at the bar, the men stood back, scanning the room.

Caleb and Juan stood in the corner. Caleb's gaze combed the crowd, looking for unattached women. Juan hung back and drank his beer, his keen eyes never resting on anyone for long. He gaze landed on April, but didn't recognize her at first.

"Hey, there's a couple of lookers at that table," Caleb said.

"Isn't that the girl we saw today at The Birches?"

"Might be. She was too far away for me to see good."

"She's not alone, Caleb."

"It's one guy for two women there. One of those two babes has to be free."

"Maybe. Don't wreck anything. Hang tight. I see a woman at the bar...she's looking this way."

Caleb's head snapped around and he eyed the blonde at the bar. A smile spread across his face when his eyes locked with hers. She returned his smile.

"You can have those two. I'm set," he said, slowly walking over to the bar.

Chapter Sixteen

Friday night, April was in a tizzy. The day had been filled with fixing many small mistakes: art filed in the wrong place, modern art hung upside down, things misplaced, people not where they were supposed to be. It seemed her cell never stopped ringing.

The weather would not cooperate as it got hot, then thunder showers rolled in, drenching visitors. The art gallery and pre-show was quickly moved inside the school.

People flooded in to the tiny communities, causing long lines at restaurants and gas stations. Hotels, motels, and B & B's were all booked solid. People were renting out rooms in their homes. Alice Green was so excited she could hardly speak as she met famous, influential people from the art and media worlds.

April's father insisted on taking her to dinner. She was exhausted and tense so she ate quickly and returned home. Thankfully, her father had behaved himself. Romeo showed up, rubbing up against her legs, an action she found soothing. She sat petting him, drinking a cup of tea on her deck.

"Are you okay?" Gavin's voice startled her.

She nodded at him with a smile. "I am now."

"Sure?

"It's been a crazy day. I've done all I can. What will be will be. Nothing left to do."

"I'm proud of what you've done." He brushed a few strands of hair from her face.

Romeo meowed for Gavin, who bent down and petted the cat. "I suppose if you moved out of here, you'd want to bring this cat with you."

"Don't know if he'd come," she said.

"He's too smart to walk away from regular meals."

"Perhaps. Why do you ask?"

"No reason...curious..."

April looked up at the moon still visible through the clouds floating. Gavin stepped closer to her.

"April...I...do you..."

"What?" she asked, turning to face him.

"Nothing. What color dress are you wearing tomorrow?"

"Red, why?"

"Wanted to get you some flowers," he said, shyly.

Her eyes filled with tears. "That's so sweet."

She took his face in her hands and kissed him. He put his hands on her waist and pulled her closer to him. He angled his head and deepened the kiss, holding her close.

"Springtime," he murmured into her hair.

April closed her eyes and absorbed his strength through his hug. A small burst of energy brightened her spirits and made her smile.

"I have to sleep. Tomorrow is almost here."

He nodded, gave her one more hug and stepped back. "What time shall I pick you up?"

"I have to be there very early, you don't need to—"

"I said, what time?"

She smiled. "Okay. Four o'clock."

"Shoot, that is early." He grinned. "I'll be here."

They kissed goodnight and he left.

She undressed and got into bed. In a surprise move, Romeo leaped up on the bed, curling into a ball at the bottom, near her feet. His presence and loud purr was what she needed to put her to sleep.

Saturday morning, April was up early, fed Romeo, and headed out to tend to last minute details. Sunny slept in, saving her energy as she and Mike were the auctioneers. With Sunny's art knowledge and Mike's experience on stage, it made sense for them to run the live auction.

April headquartered herself at the school. Her cell phone buzzed constantly and the place was a beehive of activity. Gavin double-checked the art to make sure the mountings were secure. Barney directed table and chair set up. Laura counted plates, tablecloths and other paraphernalia for the tables. The menu for the dinner was printed on a little artist's palette and propped up on a tiny easel on each table. The tickets were in the shape of palettes, too.

Alice Green was there, checking the lists and making sure everyone was assigned a table. April couldn't believe there were three hundred fifty people coming, far more than anyone dreamed of. With fifty pieces of art, that many people would assure each piece went for a good price. Alice grabbed April for a moment when she took a break to stuff a small sandwich in her mouth and pulled her into the ladies' room.

"This is the only place I can speak to you privately, April."

"What's up, Alice?"

"This event is so…so…much bigger than I thought it would be. I want to hire you right now to do this next year. We can't pay much, but you've earned a fee."

April blushed with pride and hugged Alice.

"I'm happy to help, Alice."

"So you'll do it next year?"

"Don't know where I'll be next year." April said, dropping her hands and stepping back a little.

"You have to stay in Pine Grove. We need you here."

Before April could reply, a loud knock on the door and Barney's booming voice interrupted the conversation.

"Ladies! No hiding in there! April, I need you to sign for these tables."

April was out of there before she could answer Alice's question. Where would she be next year? No time to think about that now. The rest of the day flew by and it was two o'clock before April could catch her breath.

She stood and looked back at the room, everything was in place. Most of the helpers moseyed on home and the gym settled into a peaceful silence. Gavin came up behind her, snaking his arm around her waist.

"It's coming together. I can't believe it," she said, leaning back against him.

"You did a great job."

"We all did a great job. I couldn't have done it without you, Laura, Barney, Sunny, Mike...so many people."

"Community."

"Yeah...community."

They headed to the parking lot, then disappeared back to their own homes to get ready. When April returned, Romeo was there, looking for a handout. Shirley and Hal stopped by to inquire about the event.

"Everything that can be done is. I'm free for two hours," she said, handing Romeo a treat.

"We can't wait. This is your night to shine, honey," Shirley said.

"The art'll shine, the dogs and cats will benefit...and maybe I've learned something," she said.

Taking lemonade into the living room, April stretched out on the sofa for a short rest and woke up an hour later. She hurried into the shower, dried her hair and slipped on her strapless, knee-length, red sheath. The long zipper up the back eluded April's grasp for the last three inches and struggle as she might, it remained open. Giving up on it, she slipped on her gold sandals and finished applying plenty of make-up right before Gavin knocked at the front door.

"Come in!" she called, searching for her gold shawl.

She turned around and caught her breath when she saw her "farm boy". Gavin was wearing a black suit, perfectly tailored to his physique, accentuating the broadness of his shoulders and the narrow line of his waist, a white shirt and sky blue tie. She thought he was the most handsome man in the world.

"You clean up great," she said.

Gavin stared at April with his mouth open, his gaze resting on her cleavage.

"Isn't your dress a little...low...a little...revealing...are you going like that?" His question ended on a squeak of his voice as he cleared his throat.

April looked down and blushed when she realized more was showing than should be because it was not zipped up all the way.

"Oh, no! Please, I need help," she said, turning her back to him. "Can you zip this all the way up for me?"

Gavin stepped up to her, his hands caressing her bare shoulders before they slid down to grip the zipper on her dress. He pulled it up all the way and April adjusted the bodice around her breasts, before pulling it up. He leaned down and nuzzled her neck, unable to keep his hands off the soft skin revealed by the dress. For a moment, his fingertips lightly caressed the tops of her breasts. April tingled all the way to her toes.

"Springtime..." he murmured, drinking in her fresh, sweet scent.

"Better?" She asked, taking a deep breath, trying to get her bearings.

She faced him and he took a step back to look her over.

"I've never seen a prettier woman, April. You look beautiful."

She smiled and reached for his hand.

"After you," he said, holding open the door.

The gym had been transformed into a glittering art gallery. The paintings were lined up on one side and the tables on the other. Each table sat ten people and was covered with a powder blue, pink or light green tablecloth. Fat candles graced every table along with small vases of fall flowers, mostly asters and zinnias. Glassware glistened and the plates sported a squeaky-clean shine.

The art was displayed on large, white "walls" that rose about eight feet tall. Each piece was mounted with a title, name of the artist and a number. People began arriving and drinking wine while they strolled through the aisles, admiring painting after painting, some oils, some in charcoal, some chalks but all by talented artists.

Sunny wore a silver floor-length gown. The dress did not hide the early evidence of her pregnancy, which she was proud of, so she didn't care. Mike wore a black tuxedo, tailored to his trim physique. They made a striking couple.

Sunny had her back to the door. When she turned around, she was face-to-face with her ex-husband, Brad White. April watched from a corner of the room.

"Caroline, how nice to see you," he said, kissing her hand.

"It's Sunny, remember?"

"Sorry, yes, so it is. This is quite an event you've got going here." He raised an eyebrow as his eyes scanned the room.

"It's for the A.S.P.C.A." Sunny said, straightening her spine.

"I know. Bunch of our old crowd are here."

"You alone?" She asked, unable to keep surprise out of her voice.

"What do you think?" He answered with a wry laugh.

"Of course not. How silly of me. Where is she?"

Brad pointed to a young redheaded woman, who was dressed to kill, sipping wine and looking at the art.

"She isn't you, but she'll do...for tonight, anyway."

"Some things never change. You're looking well."

"You, too, except a little heavier than when I last saw you," he said, his gaze dropping to her belly.

"Perhaps because I'm pregnant."

Brad's mouth fell open. He stood there gaping at her when Mike walked up behind her and put his hands on her waist. *Uh oh. Husband and ex in the same place.* April sipped her wine.

"Aren't you going to introduce me?" Mike whispered.

Sunny shifted her weight. April could tell her friend was uncomfortable.

"Mike Foster, this is Brad White."

"And who are you, Mike?" Brad asked, extending his hand.

"I'm her husband." Mike said, gripping Brad's hand a little too firmly.

Brad stepped back as if someone had slapped him across the face. Mike wore a sly smile, because he knew who Brad was although they hadn't met before.

"Ohhh, I see. You're the mystery man caught skinny-dipping in the lake with my wife, eh? Well congratulations on stealing this beauty from me. That doesn't happen often," Brad said.

"I didn't steal her from anyone." Mike said, his hand clenching into a fist at his side.

"Now, guys, enough, okay." Sunny put a calming palm on each man's shoulder.

"I can't wait to see your new work...Car...Sunny."

"The art is over there, Brad. I hope you like my new stuff."

"I like everything you do, dear, except divorcing me," he said, kissing her hand and moving toward the gallery.

"For two cents, I'd clock that guy..." Mike grumbled.

"He's not worth it."

"Let him be as nasty as he wants, you're mine, not his. His loss...big time," Mike said, pulling her close and planting a kiss on her lips.

April let out a breath she was holding. That went better than she had expected. A brawl at the event would have killed everything.

APRIL MOTIONED GAVIN over.

"Sunny sat my parents with your aunt and uncle at our table. I don't think I can face them all together tonight. Can you handle him—them for me?"

"Handle your father? No one can handle him, April."

"If anyone could, you could," she coaxed.

"As long as you don't mind if he ends up with a black eye by the end of the evening, then I'll take charge."

"I knew I could count on you."

Gavin went to the door, directed Laura and Barney to their table, then escorted Barbara and Martin. While he tried to smile, he didn't quite succeed and April chuckled behind her hand at the expression on his face, before returning to her job.

Even with a few mishaps, the evening was magical. All the paintings were purchased, some for much more money than expected and some for less. Sunny's paintings all brought high prices, even the one Brad bought. The auction was exciting when the bidding got hot. Mike handled everything with humor, getting people to bid each other up with his mantra: "Come on, folks. It's for charity."

Electricity played after the auction was over so people could dance. Sunny went home early, exhausted, but Mike remained to help. The profit from the ticket sales, sponsorships and auctioned paintings came to seventy thousand dollars, way more than Alice Green expected.

April had barely eaten, as she had to fix disaster after disaster, from mollifying disappointed bidders to making sure the food and drink kept moving. She, too, was tired at the end of the evening. Barbara managed to control Martin during the dinner. Laura and Barney ignored him when he made insensitive remarks but he made Gavin angry. April stopped by their table from time to time to check on everyone and make sure Gavin hadn't hit her father yet.

She understood that he feared losing her to Gavin. She heard him be aggressive with the young man, demanding to know what his plans were in life and regarding April. Gavin fended him off with good humor when he could and finally with anger, when his humor ran out.

April had realized a showdown couldn't be avoided between the two of them, and she was right. It came sooner than she expected, though. She stooped to pick up a program littering the floor behind one of the display walls when she heard her father's deep voice.

"I'll be taking April home this evening, Gavin. You can run along."

"Mr. McKenna, you're mistaken. April is my girl and I'm taking her home."

"You're her *date*, but I'm her *father*."

Gavin glared. "Then act like it and stop being such a fool."

Martin returned the hostile look but didn't reply. "Are you intending to stay the night with her?" Martin demanded.

"What business is that of yours? Honestly, you'd think a father would butt out of that part of his daughter's life when she's April's age. Don't you know when to back off?" Gavin's voice rose.

"She's...she's mine to protect." Martin responded feebly.

"Good *night*, Mr. McKenna," Gavin said, striding off to avoid a fight.

Barbara ushered Martin toward the door. April covered her face with her hand, wishing her father would disappear.

"But...April...I want—I want—"

"We'll see her tomorrow. It's raining and it's late. Let's go," Barbara said.

Sure enough, the heavens had opened up. Rain, accompanied by thunder and lightning, greeted the stragglers who didn't leave on time. Gavin opened an umbrella for April. Then he ran to his truck, getting only a bit wet. He drove slowly.

"It didn't go too well with my dad, did it?"

"Nope."

"That bad?"

He nodded. "You don't want to know."

"I'm sorry, but I'm not surprised." April focused her gaze at the passing scenery.

"Not your fault he's a jerk," Gavin ground out.

They drove the rest of the way in silence. When Gavin parked the truck, a huge bolt of lightning and loud clap of thunder startled April. She leaped into his arms as they huddled under the umbrella, waiting for a safe time to scoot down the embankment to the cabin. April spied Romeo was hiding under the table. As they got inside, the lights flickered and went out.

"Must be a tree or branch down on a power line," Gavin said, "where are your candles?"

April pulled out two flashlights and a handful of candles. They lit them in the kitchen.

Gavin took April's hand and led her into the bedroom. He placed lit candles on the nightstand and the dresser.

"See," she said, "no suitcases. The auction is over and I'm not leaving."

"I know. I was an idiot for not believing you."

"You believe me now?"

He nodded, pulling her over by the skylight. The rain clouds moved on, leaving the full moon to shine on the would-be lovers. A tender smile lifted the corners of his lips.

"What?"

He slipped his hand in his pants pocket. "April, I love you. You know that, right?"

"I do."

"I'd go anywhere with you. If you marry me, I'll move to Katmandu if you want to. I don't care where I live as long as it's with you...will you marry me?"

He opened his hand, and then opened the small box resting in his palm to show her the antique diamond and ruby ring. The many small diamonds around the band glittered in the candlelight but couldn't outdo the brilliance of the solitaire. April couldn't breathe. She hadn't expected this, rather she expected another type of proposal from him. Tears stung her eyes and emotion closed her throat.

"Well?"

She could only nod yes.

"You have to say it, Springtime."

"Yes, I will marry you," she breathed out, as a small tear escaped.

He slid the ring on her finger and took her in his arms.

"But I don't want to live in Katmandu. I want to live here, with you."

"Here? Are you sure?"

"I'm sure. I love it here. You were right. It got under my skin." She laughed as she hugged him tightly against her. "Guess I'm a country girl now."

Gavin bent down and his lips met hers. The passion of their kiss almost knocked her off her feet as her knees went weak. But he held her up, his lips crushing hers as they were swept away by their growing desire. He angled his head and teased her mouth with his tongue, tantalizing her, creating more heat, overwhelming her. April's resistance was gone. She melted to him, losing herself in his embrace, her tongue dancing with his, her breathing becoming rapid.

His hand slid up from her waist to surround her breast. She sighed with pleasure as he caressed and massaged her, slowly, lovingly. Gavin's hand found the zipper on her dress and bit by bit slipped it down, waiting for her to stop him. Overcome with her passion for him, she wanted him as much as he wanted her.

The dress slid to the floor. His eyes swept over her body clad only in black panties.

"You're beautiful," he murmured.

Gavin's hands held her closer to him, pressing her to his chest. His lips moved under her ear and slid slowly down her neck, nibbling on her tender skin as they went.

"Springtime," he muttered as he moved his hand up to cradle her breast.

His lips blazed a hot trail to her bare shoulder while her fingers fumbled with the buttons of his shirt. As she pushed Gavin's shirt off his shoulders, there was a sharp knock on the door. The lovers jumped apart, startled. April looked at the door.

"Must be Mike, checking up to make sure I'm okay. Great timing," she muttered.

"Probably your dad, making sure we're not doing exactly what we're doing."

April laughed as she grabbed her robe, folding it across her body and tying the sash. She padded barefoot to the door, twirling her new engagement ring on her finger, holding a lit candle. She opened the door as she began to talk.

"It's okay, Mike... I'm fine—"

Then she stopped as she looked into two small black eyes, glittering malevolently in the candlelight.

Chapter Seventeen

"You Rusty's girl?" the short man asked.

April stood looking at him, unable to speak. Finally, she nodded. "I was."

"Good," the dark man said, pushing past her.

April gasped at the sight of two men toting guns. For a split second she glanced at the bedroom, then away quickly so as not to betray Gavin's presence. She faked a cough to draw attention away from where he was hiding. A second man followed behind the first and closed the door. Candlelight reflected off the barrels of two Glocks pointed at April's chest.

"Where's the money?" the first man demanded.

April backed away. "What money? What are you talking about?"

"Come on, tootsie, you know what I'm talking about," said the stranger.

"She's not dressed, Juan. Ready for action, I like that," said the other man, stepping forward and moving his gun barrel toward April's robe.

April pushed it away.

"Leave her, Caleb. Give us the money, chicky, and we'll go away," said Juan.

"I don't *have* any money."

"I ain't stupid! Rusty stole sixty thousand dollars of our money. He's dead so he can't have it. Means you gotta have it. Fork it over." Juan took a step forward.

"I don't have it. Honestly. You can look around. There's no money here. Do you think I'd be living in a place like this if I had sixty thousand dollars?"

Juan shrugged. "I don't care what you say. He's dead. You were his woman. You got the money."

"Can I play with her?" asked Caleb.

Juan looked at Caleb and back at April. She instinctively held her robe closed with a shaking hand. Small droplets of sweat formed on her upper lip.

"Sure. She don't give us the money... she can give us something else, then maybe she'll give us the money."

Caleb took off his shirt. "Hot in here. Why don't you take off your robe, sweet cakes? Get comfortable." Caleb said.

April began to cry.

"Give us the money and we'll leave you alone!" Juan hollered.

"I don't have the money. I don't. Don't you think I would give it to you if I did?"

April heard a click from the bedroom.

Juan's face became wary. "What was that?" His eyes searched the room.

"What? I didn't hear anything?" she lied, recognizing the sound of the magazine being snapped into place.

Juan's little black eyes bored into her. "Well, *I* heard something. What was it?"

He poked the gun into her ribs and she started coughing, making as much noise as she could to cover the noise of the bolt sliding back.

"Okay, you've had your chance, now it's my turn," Caleb said, reaching for April.

Gavin burst out of the bedroom, firing the .22 automatic rifle at Caleb, hitting him in the shoulder. Juan raised the Glock, and aimed it at Gavin. April screamed and Gavin fired three times, hitting Juan in the chest. Juan fired the Glock once, hitting the wall before he went down. Caleb reached for his gun and Gavin plugged him in the arm.

"Kick the gun away from him, April!" Gavin ordered.

She did as he told her, sliding it along the floor away from Caleb, who was writhing in pain and screaming. Juan lay on the floor completely still. Gavin handed his phone to April while he picked up the Glock and aimed it at Caleb.

"Call Justin."

April tried to control her shaking fingers long enough to dial the phone, but was unsuccessful.

"He's the third name down," Gavin said.

She pushed the button and the phone started ringing. She handed it to Gavin.

"Justin, we've got a couple of bad guys here at April's cabin. Yeah. Ambulance, too. I think one may be dead. No, no. I shot him. Right."

Gavin closed the phone and not thirty seconds later, April heard the siren of the Sheriff's car as it raced to The Birches. She stood still, trying to take in what had happened. Gavin reached over and pulled her to him. He put his arm around her, folding her into his shoulder. The shock wore off, and she started to cry, sobbing into his chest as he held the Glock on Caleb.

Within five minutes, Justin was in the cabin. He took the Glock from Gavin and asked what happened. April quieted down.

"Get dressed you two and come down to the Sheriff's office so I can get your stories on paper," Justin said.

April went into the bedroom and closed the door. She tried to still her shaking hands long enough to slip on shorts, a T-shirt and flip flops. She grabbed Gavin's shirt and opened the door. He took the shirt from her and pulled it over his shoulders, leaving it unbuttoned, then gathered her in his arms for a tight hug.

"Are you all right?" he whispered, his breath fanning warm against her neck.

She nodded, resting her cheek against his chest. Justin took April and Gavin in the squad car while the ambulance picked up Caleb and Juan and transported them to the hospital in Willow Falls.

Justin called Cassie on the phone to tell her he'd be home late. April touched his shoulder as she looked at her ring.

"Tell Cassie, Gavin and I are engaged," she said.

Justin smiled and relayed the message.

"I didn't mean for our engagement night to go like this," said Gavin.

"You saved me...saved me in more ways than one." April nestled into his shoulder.

Sliding his arm around her, Gavin murmured in her ear. "Springtime, you're mine now, forever."

APRIL AND GAVIN SPENT several hours in the Sheriff's office, writing up their stories and waiting to hear if Juan would survive. April came clean about Rusty, his activities and about the money Juan and Caleb were seeking.

"You knew about the money?" Gavin asked April.

She looked down at the floor for a long moment then finally nodded.

"Knew what they wanted, what they were talking about?"

She nodded again, leaning against him.

"Why didn't you tell me?"

"I promised not to, besides, I didn't want to get you involved."

"That didn't work out too well, did it?" He asked her gently, cupping his hand over her cheek.

"I didn't know they knew about me, no idea they were coming here. Believe me, if I thought we were in danger, I would have told you." She said, standing up.

"We're getting married now, no more secrets."

"No more secrets but you understand, don't you?" April paced back and forth.

"Maybe, still don't like it," he said, taking her hands in his and stopping her.

About three a.m., Justin got the call from Dr. Barrow informing him Juan had died. This changed everything and new paperwork needed to be filed and new questions asked. April and Gavin remained in the sheriff's office for another hour.

"I'm sorry but you can't go back to the cabin yet," Justin said.

"Why not?" April asked.

"It's a crime scene. It'll be a few days until you can have it back."

"Can I go and pick up some clothes?"

"Sure, I can send an officer with you. But that's all."

At the cabin, Gavin wasn't allowed to enter, so April went inside with the officer. She packed a small suitcase and left food for Romeo. April stood in the parking lot and began to cry.

"Where am I going to go?"

"Don't worry about that," said Gavin.

He took her suitcase and threw it in the truck bed. Then he opened the door for April, and helped her inside.

April leaned back against the front seat of the truck and fell fast asleep. When they arrived at their destination, Gavin slid the sleeping woman out of the seat and carried her into the bedroom. The minute he laid her down on the bed, she started to stir.

"Where are we?"

"Rest. Close your eyes," Gavin said as he turned to leave.

April grabbed his hand and pulled him toward her.

"Don't leave. Stay with me."

He smiled down at her, his hand rose to stroke her cheek.

"Springtime, I can't resist you...if I get on that bed, I'm going to make love to you."

"So?" She asked, looking up into his eyes.

"You want me to...?"

"Shhh," she said, putting her finger to her lips, "No talking. Kiss me."

Gavin did as he was told. Kicking off his shoes, he knelt on the bed, lowering himself slowly down next to April. She turned to face him, bringing her mouth to his. Angling his head, Gavin increased the intensity of the kiss. April pushed his shirt off his shoulders. He let it drop, and then nodded to her.

She shed her shirt quickly then her shorts. He did the same. Gavin leaned over to kiss her again, nudging her lips open with his. Their tongues played while his fingers threaded through her hair. When April rested her hands on his bare chest a small shiver ran up her spine.

Gavin sat up, then stood up. He removed his boxers and pulled down the covers, sliding into bed. April removed her bra and panties, tossed them on the chair next to the bed, and slipped in next to him.

She turned on her side to face him. Gavin cupped her head with his hand and drew her closer, his mouth seeking hers. April touched his stubbly face while his mouth ravaged hers sending a charge surging through her veins. Putting her hand on his waist, she pulled herself flat up against him. The skin-to-skin contact sent heat throughout her body as his lips traveled down her neck to her shoulder.

Gavin eased her down on her back and pulled the sheet down, feasting his eyes on her. A wave of shyness swept through April, who sat up and tugged at the sheet.

"Let me look at you, Springtime. I've waited a long time...you're so beautiful," he whispered, his hand gently stopping her wrist.

She let go of the sheet and lay back down on the pillows. Gavin's hands caressed her from top to toe. She squirmed with the excitement he was creating and pulled him closer.

"I love you," she sighed.

"I love you, too." His hand glided over her firm behind, resting on the back of her thigh, while his lips traveled down her neck to her chest, stopping on her breast. A shiver ran up her spine.

"Take me," she whispered, running her hands up his chest and closing her eyes as the red-gold rays of sunrise peeked through the curtains.

"My pleasure, Springtime..." he murmured, before reaching over to the nightstand to flip off the light, then lowering himself into her waiting arms.

MARTIN WAS UP AT SIX and ready to pick his daughter up at seven for breakfast.

"Martin, let her sleep," Barbara said, pulling on his sleeve.

"Sleep? You think she's asleep? She's with Gavin and I doubt they're sleeping."

"Let her alone. She's a grown woman, Martin."

"She's still my daughter."

"Don't you remember when we were dating?"

"Of course I remember. I remember perfectly...and he's no different than I was."

"I couldn't resist you either and we've been married for a long time. She'll be fine. Let her rest."

Martin got behind the wheel of his car and drove over to The Birches. He was astounded to find yellow tape and a police officer outside his daughter's cabin. He called Barbara immediately.

"So did you interrupt them like you hoped to?" Barbara asked, in a sleepy voice.

"They aren't here. This is a crime scene! I don't know where she is but a crime was committed in this cabin last night. You'd better come."

Barbara dressed quickly and woke Sunny and Mike. Still tired from the big night, Sunny stayed in bed on the promise they would call her when they knew anything. Mike went with Barbara. When they arrived, Martin was practically hysterical.

"They won't tell my anything, except someone died here. Won't tell me where April is," Martin said, wringing his hands.

"I'm sorry, sir, but I don't know where you daughter is."

"Was she the victim of a crime?" Martin asked, his voice rising, his hand on the officer's shoulder.

"Don't know, sir, I arrived only half an hour ago." She said, shrugging his hand off.

"Someone died here...was it my daughter?" he asked, sinking onto a bench on the deck.

"No, sir. Not female."

"Was it Gavin?" Barbara asked, her face ashen, sliding onto the bench next to Martin.

"You'll have to talk to the Sheriff, Ma'am," the officer said, standing stiffly in front of the door.

Mike turned to Barbara, keeping his voice down,

"Maybe they're in Gavin's apartment," he said covering her ear with his hand and whispering to her.

"I heard that. Maybe they're shacking up at his place. Let's go," Martin said.

At eight o'clock, when The McKennas and Mike arrived, Barney and Laura were awake but not dressed. Martin banged on the door. It was answered quickly. He rushed in when Barney opened the door.

"Where's my daughter?"

"What?" Laura asked him, rising from the breakfast table.

"April. Where is she?" Martin asked, looking around.

"I don't have any idea," Barney said, putting down his newspaper.

"Doesn't she have her own place?" Laura asked, her brows knitted.

"She's not there," Barbara said.

"She must be here. Where is Gavin's room?" Martin asked, opening doors.

"He has an apartment upstairs, but that's his private residence. We can't go barging in there." Laura said.

"I can't...but you can. It's part of your house." Martin said, his hand on Barney's forearm.

"I'll do nothing of the sort." Barney said, gently pushing Martin's hand away .

"My daughter may be in there," Martin said, turning to Laura for help.

"Your daughter is an adult, Martin, not a minor." Laura reminded him.

"I'm not going to barge into Gavin's place on your say-so," Barney said, folding his arms across his chest.

"Could you at least knock on his door?" Barbara asked. Her gentle question calmed everyone down.

"Right—right...what she said," Martin stammered.

Barney looked skeptical, but he walked up the stairs and knocked gently on the door.

"That isn't loud enough to wake a sleeping mouse!" Martin yelled.

Barney knocked louder, but there was no answer. The silence in the living room was deafening. Barney knocked a third time, very loud. He looked at Laura and shrugged his shoulders. She shrugged back and Barney cracked the door slightly and called inside.

"Gavin! Gavin you in there, son?"

No answer.

"Oh my, they're both gone," Laura sighed, sinking into a chair.

"You sure they're not at the cabin?" Barney asked.

"The cabin is crawling with police because it's a crime scene, I'd know if my daughter was there," Martin said pacing around the room.

At that information, Laura burst into tears.

"What's the matter with you, blurting out something like that? You're an idiot, Martin," Barney said, pulling out a handkerchief and going to his wife's side.

All of a sudden everyone started talking. Laura and Barney got dressed while Barbara put on another pot of coffee. After they drank it, everyone calmed down. Then they headed to the police station.

Justin explained what had happened the night before but said he didn't know where Gavin and April were. Mike called Sunny to bring her up to date then suggested they go to lunch.

"They're fine and they're going to turn up," he assured the two families.

The group traipsed into The Luncheonette, all talking at once. Sunny met them there.

"That Rusty was no good, I knew it from the start," Martin said.

"Doesn't matter now, does it? He's gone and our children have been threatened," Laura said.

"Who knows how many other members there were in this gang? Maybe they're out for revenge. Maybe they took Gavin and April," Barney said.

Everyone went silent, contemplating Barney's suggestion.

"I don't think we should go off the deep end here. There must be a logical explanation," Mike said.

Sunny dialed April's cell phone but got no response. Laura dialed Gavin's phone and got no response either. The group spent the afternoon trying to come up with a plan to find their children but by dinner time, they were still missing.

"I suggest we go home and wait. They will contact us when they want to," Sunny said.

While they grumbled, everyone was tired so they disbanded.

"I hope April is all right," Laura said to Barbara, giving her a hug.

"Same goes for Gavin," Barbara said.

They hugged each other and parted, making a plan to meet at The Luncheonette in the morning at eight am for breakfast.

When they met in the morning, no one looked well rested. Big circles showed under Martin's eyes indicating his sleepless night. The group gathered no new information to share and were quiet and subdued for a change, lost in their own thoughts.

"Gavin saved April, according to the Sheriff. I forgot to thank you for that," Martin said to Laura.

"Don't thank us, thank Gavin," she replied.

Martin nodded. Just when everyone ran out of ideas, Justin walked in. He sat in the corner and ate his breakfast quietly. When he was finished, he approached the group.

"What I'm going to say doesn't apply to Sunny and Mike, but it does to the rest of you. You don't deserve to know where they are. When I last saw them they were fine. I have an idea where they might be. I'll take you there, though it's against my better judgment."

They piled into their cars and followed Justin, who drove through town and down to the back acres of the Dailey property. Gavin's log home sat proudly in the middle of a clearing. The curtains were shut and the house seemed deserted. Justin got out of his car and walked around back.

"Gavin's truck is parked out back," he said.

Smiles began to spread on faces.

"Careful what you say to them, now," Justin warned, "I'm prepared to file a justifiable homicide charge if Gavin shoots any one of you."

They looked at each other, but no one mustered the courage to go and knock on the door. Sunny finally did the deed. Nothing happened. She knocked again.

"Coming. Keep your pants on," Gavin's voice floated through the door.

Everyone crowded around the front steps as the door opened slowly. Gavin stood there wearing only a pair of jeans. He looked at everyone with a jaundiced eye.

"Where's my—" Martin started but stopped.

April, tying the sash of her short robe, moved around from behind Gavin to stand next to him. It was obvious she wasn't dressed and nervous sounds came from the older adults. Sunny and Mike could barely keep the smiles from their faces as they stepped back slowly. Gavin put his arm around April.

"What do y'all want?" he asked.

"Are you shacking up with my daughter?" Martin brazened.

"Do you mean am I shacking up with my *wife?* Damn right I am," he snickered.

April took her left hand and waved it in front of their faces. Everyone gasped as they spied the wedding ring she wore. She picked up Gavin's and showed his wedding ring to them, too.

"Oh my, you're married?" Barbara asked, feebly.

April nodded, then stepped next to Gavin and wound her arms around his waist.

"Anyone have a problem with that?" Gavin asked. His arm resting on April's shoulders.

No one made a sound.

"I'm disappointed we didn't get to be there, son," Laura said.

"Me, too, Aunt Laura. But the way you all were acting...we went to Judge Fitch and he married us."

"How could I have had you there, Dad?" April asked, looking directly at her father.

Martin looked at the ground.

"I always thought...your wedding..." Barbara said, tears filling her eyes.

"I'm sorry, Mom. You gave us no choice. Dad, you won't accept I don't want to go back to San Francisco. I'm not going back. Gavin and I are going to live here. I love it here. People are nice to me. Alice Green has offered to pay me to do the art auction next year and the mayor asked me to arrange a music festival here next summer, too."

"We love each other, Mr. McKenna," Gavin said.

"Martin," he said, extending his hand.

"Okay...Martin. I'm going to take care of April. You never have to worry about her. But right now, we need to be only us for a while." Gavin said, shaking Martin's hand briefly.

April let go of her husband and the newlyweds went back inside and closed the door.

SUNNY AND MIKE RETURNED home, leaving the parents to commiserate at the Dailey's house. Laura fixed lunch and they got along.

"We're related now, I guess," Martin said.

"Like it or not," Barney sighed.

"I apologize for everything. I got us into this and I'm sorry. Gavin saved April's life, I'm sure he's a fine man and a good choice." Martin announced.

"April seems very happy with him," Barbara concurred.

They all nodded.

"We forgive you, Martin," Laura said, giving him a hug.

They started planning a party for April and Gavin.

"If we can't throw a wedding, at least we can have a party," Barbara said.

Later that afternoon, they drove back over to the log home. Barney and Laura put out dishes covered in plastic wrap so Gavin and April wouldn't have to cook. Martin left an envelope. They knocked on the door then left.

IT TOOK GAVIN A WHILE to open the door but he was delighted to find the food. He handed the envelope to April. She opened it and read the letter aloud to Gavin:

To my beloved April,

I guess I made a mess of this. I'm sorry. Gavin seems like a fine man. He

was there when you needed him, which is more than most. I will miss walking you

down the aisle and giving you away, though this may be less painful for me.

> *You'll always be my little girl. Enclosed is a check for the money I would have spent on your wedding. Use it for whatever you need. It comes from your mother and me with much love and hope for your forgiveness and Gavin's. Wishing a long and happy life together for you both.*

Love,

Dad

P.S. We have already made plane reservations to come here for Thanksgiving.

April took out the check. It was made out for ten thousand dollars. She whooped with joy and showed it to Gavin.

"Do you think you can ever forgive my father?" April asked him.

"Driven to distraction by his love for you…let me see…can I identify with that?" Gavin stroked his chin thoughtfully and laughed. "Guess I can. Can you?"

"Eventually."

"Better get over it by Thanksgiving," he warned.

"Oh my, only two and a half months to get ready."

Gavin pulled her over to the skylight in the bedroom. She moved up into his arms, against his chest.

"What did you once tell me you learned in Paris?" She asked, her eyes teasing him, her hands on his shoulders.

Gavin laughed and pulled her closer, lowering his lips to hers.

"Time for April's kiss in the moonlight," he said.

** THE END**

Keep reading for a taste of the *Under the Midnight Moon*, the next story in this series. You'll meet April's college roommate, Mindy Winslow.

Chapter One

Mindy Winslow awoke to a hand shaking her shoulder. She rubbed her eyes then opened them to peer into a pair of gorgeous, masculine, blue greens. Her gaze traveled down to his shoulders. *Maybe as wide as the Delaware River?* Then to his left hand. *No ring. Unmarried or gay?*

"Ms. Winslow?"

"That's me. We're here already?" She glanced out the window of the bus and sat up, smoothing the wrinkles out of her sexy sweater.

"Drew Armstrong. Lou's attorney. I sent you a letter?" He extended his hand, and Mindy shook it. *Strong grip but not crushing.*

"Oh, yeah. I have it with me."

"Welcome to Pine Grove."

She tingled as the warmth from his gaze moved down her body. *How long will it take his stare to get to my breasts?* She noticed a slight flush in his neck as his eyes paused at her chest before returning to her face. *Didn't take you long, handsome.* Smiling up at him, she pushed to her feet to follow when he walked quickly down the aisle.

"Luggage?" He asked her.

She nodded at a red suitcase standing on the sidewalk where the bus driver had left it. Drew picked it up.

"This way." He pointed toward a black SUV parked at the curb.

No one has carried my luggage since I left home for New York. I could get used to this.

Drew opened the door for her before loading her suitcase in the back. Mindy slid in and closed the door. Before he slipped the key in the ignition, he turned to her, "We have a little time before Lou's funeral. Have you eaten?"

She shook her head.

"How about we grab lunch then head over there? Afterward, I'll take you wherever you're staying."

"I'm staying with April McKenna's in-laws."

Mindy looked out the window. The view was gray as only a November day in upstate New York could be. The trees were bare—their dead leaves gone brown on the ground swirled up into mini tornadoes as the wind picked up. Even in tiny Pine Grove, traffic was thick the Saturday before Thanksgiving, slowing their progress.

"You're going to be here for the wedding?" He put the car in gear and pulled out of the bus station parking lot.

"April is my college roommate. I'm...uh, a bridesmaid." She laughed.

A funeral and a wedding on the same day. What do you wear? Black? White? Black and white? Change in the car? If it wasn't so sad, it would be funny. Lou is probably laughing wherever he is.

"I'm going to the wedding, too."

"Small world."

"In Pine Grove, it's always a small world." He chuckled as he turned the car into the parking lot at Homer's, the only restaurant in town.

HOMER ANTHONY, THE owner, greeted Drew with a handshake and seated them at a table by a window overlooking the lake. Mindy glanced at the dark water. "So this is Lou's beloved Cedar Lake he always talked about."

Lou never told me she looked like this. Drew smiled at her. His gaze took in her long hair, so dark it appeared to be black. Almost transparent ice-blue eyes were startling in their beauty. Since Mindy's attention was focused on the lake, he checked out her body. First stop, the scooped neck of her sweater, which revealed enough cleavage to hold his attention. *Nice, at least a handful...maybe more.*

"It's frozen. Can you skate there?"

Drew snapped back to her face. "It can be dangerous, especially in a warmer winter. Hard to know how deep the ice actually is."

She shifted in her seat. *Small waist, generous hips. Hate a tiny-hipped woman in bed. Nothing to grab onto.* He leaned slightly to the left, hoping she didn't notice him checking out her rear end. *Can't see much while she's in the chair, but from here it looks perfect.*

Mindy dug a lipstick out of her purse, drawing his eyes to her lips as she slowly reapplied the pink color. His mouth went dry as he followed the trail over her sensuous lower lip. He wondered what it would feel like to have them pressed against his.

"What's good here?" She asked, picking up the menu before looking at him.

"They make a great blue cheeseburger." Food was the last thing on his mind.

"Hmm. Haven't had one of those in an age. Fattening, but I didn't have breakfast, so maybe I'll splurge."

The waitress arrived to fill their water glasses. Drew ordered two blue cheeseburgers with fries and *Cokes.*

"Your return address says Oak Bend. Do you live there, too?"

"I live in Pine Grove, but work in Oak Bend."

"How come? I'd think the benefit of being out here in the boonies is that you can live and work in the same town."

"I found a small house here real cheap. I'm fixing it up with Gavin's help." He unfolded his napkin and put it in his lap.

"You own a house? So great to own a house." She sat back, a smile lighting up her face.

"Be careful what you wish for..."

She cocked her head slightly. "What do you mean?"

"You'll know soon enough." A Cheshire Cat grin stretched his lips.

Mindy cocked an eyebrow at him.

"What do you do for a living?" He took a sip from his water glass.

"I'm an administrative assistant in an accounting firm. But my passion is the theater."

My passion is quickly becoming you and the law. "What exactly do you do in the theater?"

"I've written a play. I like to direct, produce...anything that connects me...it's like it's in my blood. I've been working in experimental theater on weekends, hoping to get a break."

The waitress brought their food. Mindy's eyes lit up as she gazed at the giant, juicy burger. Drew picked up his and took a healthy bite. Mindy cut hers in half before attempting to eat.

"I've never seen anyone do that before," Drew commented.

"I grew up with two big brothers...slobs, both of them. My mom and I are dainty eaters."

"So where are you from, originally? New York City?"

She laughed. "I guess I look New York by now. I come from a small town upstate. My dad has a dairy farm with my two brothers."

"Your family must miss you, being so far away."

"My dad wanted me to stay and help out on the farm...get married and settle down there. He never understood how I feel about the theater. We've lost touch. Everyone's lives get so busy and all..." Her voice trailed off, and her gaze fell to her plate.

They ate in silence for a few minutes. *Now that Lou's gone, she's all alone. Pretty young to be completely on her own. Maybe she'll stay here? There aren't any women like her here.*

"What about you? Where are you from?"

"I'm from Washington, D.C., one of five kids. I went to law school at Kensington State and got an internship at a firm in Oak Bend. After graduation, they offered me a job. So I stayed. Now I'm a partner. It's a small firm but that gives me more freedom. I get to do lots of different things instead of the same stuff all the time."

"You're settled here?"

He took another bite of his burger and nodded.

"How's the single life up here...or is that too personal?" Embarrassment at her bold question brought pink to her cheeks. *Even more beautiful when she blushes.*

"It stinks. We sure don't have women up here who look like you," he blurted out. *Idiot! Shut the hell up. Smooth, real smooth. Why don't you just ask her to take off her clothes and lie on the floor? Jerk!*

Mindy laughed, relieving some of Drew's discomfort. "Thanks."

The waitress showed up with the check, giving Drew something to do. Mindy reached for her purse, but he put up his hand to stop her. "Please, it's on me." He reached into his back pocket for his wallet.

"I don't even know you."

"Lou would want it that way." He pulled out some bills and tossed them on the table.

"Yeah, that's Lou." Sadness returned to her eyes.

Why can't you shut up? She's sad again. What's wrong with you? You're not usually this stupid in front of women.

DREW'S SUV PULLED UP in front of a small white church.

"A church? Lou was never religious," Mindy said before she opened the car door.

"Maybe not, but he had some old friends who belong here, and we needed a place to have this, so..."

She nodded, following him to the front door. Her gaze traveled his length from the back, where he couldn't see her checking him out. *Slim hips, thighs almost straining against his suit pants, and those shoulders knock me out. Blond hair, short and neat...just right. He must work out. Oh, man, a cute butt, too.*

Drew opened the big, painted wooden doors and stepped aside, allowing her to pass first. Musty air and silence surrounded them. The solemn quiet sent a tremor of pain and sadness shooting through her body. Mindy raised her eyes to the end of the aisle, her gaze zeroing in on a fancy urn. Clutching a pew to steady herself, a lightheaded feeling stopped her. *Lou's ashes!* She tightened her grip on the wooden bench while her thoughts returned to the day Lou died.

"Brian! Lou's here for the rent," Mindy called through the bathroom door.

"Can he come back? I have two shoots this week."

"He can't come back. The rent is due...it's always due this time, every month."

"As regular as you are," Brian snickered through the closed door.

"Very funny! Get your butt out here. How much do you have?"

"Half."

"I'll spot you, but you'd better pay me back next week."

"I promise." The door opened, and Brian bent down to kiss her cheek.

Grumbling to herself, Mindy returned to the living room. "Lou, Brian will be right out. He's only got half, but I'm—"

She stopped when she saw her seventy-year-old landlord slumped on the sofa with his eyes closed. "Very funny, Lou. Come on, wake up. I'm going to chip in the difference."

Mindy leaned over and shook his shoulder. He didn't move. "Lou...enough with the practical jokes..." She shoved him harder, and the man fell over in a heap.

"Brian!" Mindy screamed. "Brian!" She kept screaming until he came running.

"He's not moving, Bri...he's not moving!" Her voice shook.

Brian picked up Lou and set him back against the sofa cushions. "Call 911, Mindy." He put his two fingers against Lou's neck. Mindy dialed the number with a trembling hand while tears pricked at the backs of her eyes.

"I think he's gone, honey. I think he's gone." Brian's voice was soft.

"No!" She shouted before tears poured down her cheeks.

Drew was at Mindy's side right away. "Are you all right?"

She nodded weakly. He placed a large, steady hand under her elbow and escorted her to the first row. Limp, she sank into the seat. Rooting around for a tissue, she couldn't find the small packet she'd bought at the bus station in the city. A masculine hand gently shaking a handkerchief caught her attention. "Mom always made us boys take these. Now I know why." He smiled at her.

Mindy returned his grin with a grateful lifting of the corners of her mouth as she took the cloth from him. Drew claimed the seat next to her moments before a minister entered from a door camouflaged as a panel. An organist piped up from an instrument hidden behind a screen, and Lou's favorite Beethoven sonata filled the air. Mindy tried to concentrate on the words the minister was saying, but she couldn't focus. Unable to tear her gaze away from the urn that held the remains of her friend of six years, pain stabbed at her heart.

At one point, the man talking stopped. He introduced a few people who stepped up to the podium and said a few words about Lou. These were his oldest friends, friends from his childhood and early adult years in Pine Grove. There was a pause, then she heard her name mentioned.

"He wants you to come and say a few words," Drew whispered in her ear. "Do you feel up to it?"

She smoothed the badly wrinkled paper she had been folding and refolding in her lap while the others spoke. Unfolding it one more time, she put her hand on the armrest and pushed herself into an upright position. One knee started to shake, and she thought she was going to fall to the floor until Drew took her arm. He escorted her up to the podium, then stepped back, waiting for her to speak.

"Lou Chambers was like a father to me. He took me in when I had no money and gave me a place to live. He helped me get a job. Lou believed in me when no one else did. He encouraged me, listened to me...read my script for hours and hours, revision after revision. Lou always had time for me, no matter what.

"He had a tradition of coming for dinner on Mondays, the day the theaters are closed. I learned how to cook some great things for those visits. Learning is a word that comes to mind when I think of him…he taught me how to fill out a job application, file my income taxes, bake bread, and be…an independent person. The other word that comes to mind is *love*. I loved Lou."

Her chin quivered, and she stopped to take a deep breath. "I may have been the daughter he never had, but he was the father I always wanted. I'll miss you, Lou, and I'll never forget the things you taught me." Tears streaked down her face. She gripped the podium for dear life—so tight the tips of her fingers turned white—as she held herself upright. Drew stepped forward to take her arm when the door in the back burst open and a devastatingly handsome, breathless young man rushed up the aisle. Mindy looked up. "Brian!"

He took Mindy in his arms for a hug. Drew stood still while Brian escorted the trembling young woman back to her seat. Once seated, Brian kept hold of her hand as she dabbed her face with Drew's handkerchief. Mindy's was the last speech. The minister droned on about there being a reception at Mary McGinty's house, but Mindy wasn't listening. Sadness rocketed through her body, paralyzing her. With one young man on each side of her, Mindy slowly regained her composure. Mourners arose and filed slowly out of the church. When the church emptied out, only the three young people remained.

"I'm sorry I didn't get here sooner. Did I miss anything?"

Mindy shook her head. "Brian Kirby, Drew Armstrong." Mindy waved her hand from one to the other and back again.

"Do you want to go to the reception? I can drive you and your boyfriend…" Drew offered.

"Boyfriend?" Brian let out a laugh.

"He's more likely to be your boyfriend than mine. Brian is my roommate. He's gay." Mindy pushed to her feet.

Drew let out a breath. "Offer still stands. Where do you want to go?"

"I have a wedding to attend tonight...and you, Brian?" She turned to face him.

"I couldn't miss Lou's funeral, so Giorgio drove me up. He's outside. We're staying in a bed and breakfast tonight, then driving back tomorrow."

Mindy took his hand. "I'm so glad you're here."

"Gotta shove off, you know how impatient Gee gets." He drew her into his arms for another hug.

"It's okay. You came...that's all that matters." She kissed his cheek. "Drew? Would you mind taking me to April's?"

"Of course." Drew extended his hand to Brian, who shook it while giving the good-looking attorney the once over.

"Straight as an arrow, aren't you?"

Drew laughed and nodded.

"Damn! He's all yours, Mindy." Brian leaned over to kiss her once more, then was gone as quickly as he had arrived.

Drew took her elbow, escorting her slowly toward the door. She eyed his handkerchief, crumpled into a ball held tightly in her fist. "Oh, my. I'll wash this and get it back to you."

"No rush." He opened the car door for her.

Glancing at her before he put the car in gear, Drew broached a new topic. "I'd like to do the reading of the will at ten tomorrow, even though its Sunday, if that's okay with you. Think you're up to it?"

"Might as well get it out of the way," she sighed, shifting her gaze to the bleak scenery.

"There's a lot to go over in the next week, so we should get started tomorrow...since Thursday's Thanksgiving and all."

"No problem."

As he pulled the SUV out of the parking lot, heading to April and Gavin's house, Drew spoke up. "Brian's your roommate?"

"And best friend. Don't let his looks fool you, Brian is a very talented actor. He models while he waits for acting jobs. We've been collaborating on a play."

"Collaborators and roommates, like, you sleep in the same bed with him?" Drew's eyes widened.

"No, no...we share a two bedroom apartment," Mindy chuckled.

"Didn't mean to pry..."

"Yes you did. It's okay." Mindy turned her gaze to the side window. "Is it far to April's place? Only four hours until her wedding. She'll be wondering where I am."

"We're almost there." Drew kept his eyes on the road.

"She's already legally married, you know."

"Everyone in town knows they eloped because their families were a pain in the butt."

"This should be some wedding." Mindy shivered.

"They're getting married at Homer's."

"Good, they can clean up if a food fight breaks out."

Drew chuckled as he threw the car in park.

The front door opened, and April McKenna Dailey came running out of the log cabin. Mindy scooted out of the car as fast as she could. Gavin stood in the doorway, grinning, watching the two women shriek with joy and hug each other. Gavin nodded to Drew, who returned the gesture.

"Ready to face this?" Drew asked his friend.

"Not sure, but it's planned, so we're going through with it. Just happy we're already married, so if the fur starts flyin', it won't matter," he chuckled.

Mindy and April walked arm-in-arm up the stairs and into the house, followed by the men.

"You never told me Mindy was so...so..." Drew began.

"Hell, I never met her before. She's something, isn't she?"

"Are you kidding? She's...awesome."

The men laughed.

April had hot Chai tea and homemade scones ready for them. The four sat down at their dining room table. April served the refreshments, chattering away at Mindy about the wedding details.

Drew bit into a cranberry scone. "This is delicious."

"Laura's recipe," April said.

Mindy shot a quizzical look at her friend.

"Gavin's aunt. You'll get to know them 'cause you're going to be staying there. Our guest room isn't ready yet, and they have a comfortable apartment on their third floor. I hope you don't mind."

"Sounds wonderful. Besides, tonight is your wedding night!"

They all laughed.

"I'll run you over there if you want," Drew offered.

"Do you know them?"

"Everyone knows Laura and Barney Dailey. And I mean that in a good way."

"Sure." *I think he likes me. My date for the wedding? Beginning to look like it.*

Once in the car, Mindy took the opportunity to get the lowdown on the wedding problems. "So why are they getting married again? April never said anything, just that she eloped. Then she said her dad and mom were throwing her a real wedding now. I don't get it."

"Seems like Laura and Barney and April's folks didn't get along. Fighting like cats and dogs, so April and Gavin decided to get married on their own and not wait for them to get their act together."

"Gotta give them credit." Mindy took in the scenery.

"I do. I'd never let anyone's family get in the way of marrying a woman I loved."

Her head snapped around. She stared at him. "Ever been engaged?"

"Not yet," he admitted, turning onto Lake Drive

"Me, neither. I'm happy on my own." She turned the car heater up slightly.

"Oh?" He glanced at her then back at the road.

"I date and stuff...but I'm in no hurry to march to the tune of a man. I had enough of that with my father and brothers."

"I hardly think of marriage as 'marching to the tune of a man'."

"Then what is it for a woman?" She faced him.

"A loving, give-and-take relationship."

"What fairytales are you reading?" She cocked an eyebrow at him.

"Look at April and Gavin." He slowed the vehicle to make a turn.

"They're the exception."

"Then I plan to be an exception, too. I like what they have."

Mindy sat quietly staring at him. *God, he's making my stomach knot just looking at him. Loving relationship? If Gavin can do it, maybe he can, too. What the hell do I care? I'm moving on in a couple of days.*

"And what exactly do they have?"

Drew pulled into the Dailey's driveway. "We'll have to continue this later. Can I pick you up tonight?"

"You asking to be my date for the wedding?" She threw the blunt question at him.

"Guess so...yeah." He blushed.

"Wedding's at six. Come get me at five," she said before opening the car door.

"Got it." Drew lugged her suitcase up on the front porch and rang the bell. Mindy smelled several mouth-watering aromas wafting from the house. Drew sniffed the air. "Laura's one of the best cooks in town, probably in the whole county."

"Smells like it."

The door was opened by a large man in his early sixties with a full head of gray hair. He wore overalls and a big smile. "You must be Mindy. April's been chattering on about you for weeks. Come on in. Can I help you with that, Drew?"

"Thanks, Barney, I got it."

Mindy stepped across the threshold and was immediately enveloped in warmth. The house had the sugary scent of luscious baked goods. The hot oven had warmed the house more than usual for country houses in November. She removed her jacket and looked around. The neat living room was spacious yet cozy. With over-stuffed chairs and a sofa—covered in floral prints with a touch of blue to match the walls—the exceptionally tidy room looked inviting.

"Right this way," Barney said, showing Drew the door to the upstairs apartment.

Laura, a slim, tall woman in her early sixties with white hair, joined them. She wore a gingham apron and wiped her hands on a dish towel as she approached.

"So much to do for this shindig," she muttered. "You must be Mindy?"

Mindy extended her hand, but Laura grasped the young woman in a warm embrace instead.

"Any dear friend of April's is like family to us. Welcome, Mindy."

Tears stung the back of Mindy's eyes. Their warmth and friendliness overwhelmed her. *I wish this was my family.* She tried to form words, but the lump gathering in her throat made speech impossible. She resorted to a wide grin and a nod.

"Come on, come see the apartment. I think you'll like it."

She followed the older woman up a steep flight of stairs that led right into the apartment living room. This one was smaller, but also cheerful in peach and yellow with a comfortable-looking sofa and two wing chairs. Laura showed her the small Pullman kitchen, then the bedroom, decorated in lavender and cream. *Oh my God, this is like a little enchanted cottage in a fairy land somewhere. Or a set for a play.*

"I hope you'll be comfortable here. Please stay as long as you like."

"This is lovely, Mrs. Dailey..."

"Everyone calls me Laura."

"So incredibly charming, Laura, I'll never want to leave."

"We'd love to have you for a long while. We miss having Gavin up here. The patter of big feet," Laura said, then laughed at her own joke.

"This looks great. Thank you for having me."

Drew put her suitcase in the bedroom, then they all marched back downstairs.

"I'm sorry but I have a ton to do for the wedding, so please excuse me," Laura said before returning to the kitchen.

"I'm first in the shower, according to Laura's schedule. I'd better go now so there's enough hot water," Barney said before departing.

Drew checked his watch. "I'm wearing a suit. Got my jacket in the car, so I'm ready to go. I'd guess you've got some work to do."

"Work? Do you think it's work to make myself presentable?" Mindy put her hands on her hips.

"No, no, I didn't mean…"

"Then what did you mean?"

"I only meant women take a while…"

"Oh? So now it's women…all women or just ugly old me?"

"You, ugly?" He started to laugh. "You're the prettiest woman I've ever seen."

Silence fell on the room. Drew's cheeks colored. He headed for the door.

"Really?" She asked, pulling on his arm.

"Don't you look in the mirror? Do you need me to tell you what everyone in the world can see?"

"You don't have to get huffy. It's not every day I get a compliment like that."

"Well…it should be," he said. He leaned down and kissed her lightly on the lips.

"What was that for?" She ran her tongue over her bottom lip.

"Break the ice. Then the goodnight kiss won't be the first." Desire flickered briefly in his eyes, his smile wide.

Mindy blew out a breath.

"See you at five," Drew said before closing the front door behind him.

Mindy almost ran up the steps. *Damn, I've only got an hour and a half!*

TO GET THE BOOK RIGHT now on Amazon, or in Kindle Unlimited click here:

THE SERIES

OR, GET THE 3-BOOK series boxed set:

https://www.amazon.com/dp/B01MDSEJMG

About the Author

Jean Joachim is an award-winning, USA Today best-selling romance author whose books have hit the Amazon Top 100 list in the U.S. and abroad since 2012. She writes sports romance, small town romance, big city romance, and romantic suspense.

Jean has over 50 books in ebook, print and audio. She writes full-time, never far from her secret stash of black licorice. An avid bird and dog fan, she has a fondness for chickadees and pugs. A music lover, especially classical, she's married, has two grown sons and lives in New York City. She'd love to hear from you, email her at: sunnydaysbook@gmail.com

To receive news of private sales, new releases, and cover reveals, subscribe to my monthly newsletter using this link: https://landing.mailerlite.com/webforms/landing/k3p5e9

Jean has 57+ books, novellas and short stories published. Find them here: http://www.jeanjoachimbooks.com. Chat with Jean in her Facebook group, JJ's Book Buddies. Join here: https://www.facebook.com/groups/489790604419710/

Don't miss out!

Visit the website below and you can sign up to receive emails whenever Jean C. Joachim publishes a new book. There's no charge and no obligation.

https://books2read.com/r/B-A-MDPF-IYEV

BOOKS 2 READ

Connecting independent readers to independent writers.

www.ingramcontent.com/pod-product-compliance
Lightning Source LLC
Chambersburg PA
CBHW070936190726

48292CB00004B/1203